IVAN STOOD S... ...

His face was twisted with pain, but his eyes were as mean as the twin barrels of a loaded shotgun. And despite his broken toes, he threw himself at Longarm with a demented fury. Custis was expecting a rush and he anticipated that, like most muscle-bound men, Ivan would be slow. He was right and it was easy enough to step aside as the liveryman lumbered past. Longarm did not waste the opportunity to smash Ivan in the side of his ponderous jaw, knocking him back to the ground.

"I'm going to kill you," the giant said, crawling to his bare feet and trying to keep his weight off his broken toes.

DON'T MISS THESE
ALL-ACTION WESTERN SERIES
FROM THE BERKLEY PUBLISHING GROUP

THE GUNSMITH by J. R. Roberts

Clint Adams was a legend among lawmen, outlaws and ladies. They called him . . . the Gunsmith.

LONGARM by Tabor Evans

The popular long-running series about Deputy U.S. Marshal Long—his life, his loves, his fight for justice.

SLOCUM by Jake Logan

Today's longest-running action Western. John Slocum rides a deadly trail of hot blood and cold steel.

BUSHWHACKERS by B. J. Lanagan

An action-packed series by the creators of Longarm! The rousing adventures of the most brutal gang of cutthroats ever assembled—Quantrill's Raiders.

DIAMONDBACK by Guy Brewer

Dex Yancey is Diamondback, a Southern gentleman turned con man when his brother cheats him out of the family fortune. Ladies love him. Gamblers hate him. But nobody pulls one over on Dex . . .

WILDGUN by Jack Hanson

The blazing adventures of mountain man Will Barlow—from the creators of Longarm!

TEXAS TRACKER by Tom Calhoun

Meet J. T. Law: the most relentless—and dangerous—manhunter in all Texas. Where sheriffs and posses fail, he's the best man to bring in the most vicious outlaws—for a price.

TABOR EVANS

IN PARADISE

JOVE BOOKS, NEW YORK

This is a work of fiction. Names, characters, places, and incidents either
are the product of the author's imagination or are used fictitiously,
and any resemblance to actual persons, living or dead, business
establishments, events, or locales is entirely coincidental.

LONGARM IN PARADISE

A Jove Book / published by arrangement with
the author

PRINTING HISTORY
Jove edition / December 2002

Copyright © 2002 by Penguin Putnam Inc.

Visit our website at
www.penguinputnam.com

ISBN: 0-515-13419-8

A JOVE BOOK®
Jove Books are published by The Berkley Publishing Group,
a division of Penguin Putnam Inc.,
375 Hudson Street, New York, New York 10014.
JOVE and the "J" design
are trademarks belonging to Penguin Putnam Inc.

PRINTED IN THE UNITED STATES OF AMERICA

10 9 8 7 6 5 4 3 2 1

Chapter 1

When Longarm received the letter from his Arizona lawman friend, Monty Kilpatrick, he stuffed it into the inside pocket of his fashionably cut jacket and went about his usual Saturday business, which involved getting a haircut, shave and meeting a few friends to play billiards down at Chancy's Saloon. It wasn't until late that afternoon, after he'd taken a short nap and was preparing to call upon his latest girlfriend, Miss Rosie LaPlante, that he remembered the letter and sat down in his small and somewhat cluttered little hotel room and opened it, expecting the usual cheerful news that Monty wrote several times a year.

However, this letter was a shock, and the very first line caused his brow to furrow with concern and for him to whisper, "Damn!"

Taking a deep breath, Longarm read the letter out loud.

> *"Dear Custis, I am sorry to be writing to you on my deathbed but I have no other friend that I can trust or turn to in this time of great need. I have been ambushed and the doctor tells me that I will not recover from my gut wound. The best that I can do is to hold on until you arrive in the hope that I*

*can see you one last time and ask you to search for
my long-missing wife and son.*

*I am sure that Henrietta is still in Arizona, per-
haps in the low desert country with our son, who I
have not seen since he was one year old. I have
some things that I want Tyler to have from the father that he never knew. I also have a letter for him
explaining why his mother left me and asking him
to forgive us both. Henrietta and I should never
have married. I didn't treat her right, but I have
learned from my mistakes and have always dreamed
that we might one day be reunited with our boy.
Now, with me carrying lead in my festering gut, it's
clear that ain't gonna happen.*

*Custis, I have no one else to turn to who would
find my lost lady for me. Please don't let me down.
I saved your life once, so I guess you could say I'm
calling on that debt. Bury me cheap and give what
funds I have in the bank to Tyler and tell him not
to grow up to become a miserable old bachelor lawman and fool like his dead father.*

*Hurry to Mountain City, for I do not have many
days or weeks left on this earth. Your friend, Monty*

Longarm reread the letter two more times before he
carefully folded it up and put it back in his inside coat
pocket. He bit his lower lip and felt as if someone had
also shot him in the gut. He walked heavily over to his
liquor cabinet and poured a water glass full of whiskey,
then he lit a cigar and went out on the front porch of his
hotel room and sat down in a wicker rocking chair. On
the street below, men passed whistling, talking, cussing
and laughing, but he didn't notice. A skittish buggy horse
reared up and was knocked down by the rear wheel of a
big supply wagon. The horse tangled itself up in its har-
ness and caused quite a commotion. Normally, Longarm
would have hurried down his front porch stairs and as-

sisted the driver but . . . again, so deep was his grief and shock that he was oblivious to the drama as he smoked, sat in the rocking chair and stared with unseeing eyes at the city of Denver.

"Marshal? Marshal? Are you all right?"

Longarm was stirred from his grief by a firm tap on his shoulder. He looked up to see the owner of the hotel, Oliver Maples, looking down at him with grave concern. Longarm drained his glass feeling no better than he had when he'd started on the whiskey. "What?"

"You've been sitting here for over an hour, and when that horse went down . . . well, it's not like you to just do nothing."

Longarm looked down at his right hand and saw that his cigar was a stub about to burn his fingers. He hurled the stub into the street and said, "Oliver, I just got a letter from an old friend of mine who is dying in Arizona."

"A cancer?"

"A bullet to the gut. Very, very painful and often a slow death."

"I'm sorry to hear that," Oliver said with obvious sincerity. "How old was he?"

"I don't know. About my age. He was a lawman and once saved my life out in the Arizona Territory. Monty was a good man who made some mistakes early in his life and just never quite got around to fixing them. Now, he wants me to do the fixin'."

Maples nodded. "A death bed request, huh?"

"Yep."

"You gonna go out there and do it?"

"I got to," Longarm said. "I couldn't live with myself if I ignored his request and just went about my own business."

"Who murdered him?" Oliver asked, taking the rocking chair next to Longarm.

"I don't know. Maybe Monty doesn't even know. But you can bet I'll find out. Monty also wants me to find his wife and kid."

3

Oliver was well into his sixties and had thick, gray eyebrows which now shot up in disbelief. "You mean some son of a bitch murdered your friend and then ran off with his wife and kid!"

"No," Longarm said. "Henrietta took their boy and ran away with a gambling man many years ago."

"And your lawman friend didn't even go after them?"

Longarm shook his head. "Monty was hurt and humiliated and kept expecting Henrietta to come home. But she never did, and by the time my friend realized she never would, it was too late."

"Sounds like he let his pride get the best of him."

"It did." Longarm drew another cigar from his coat pocket. He bit off the tip, spit it into the busy street below and shoved it unlit into his mouth. "You see, Oliver, a lawman in a small frontier town can't ever afford to be considered weak, or sentimental or flawed. If Monty had of gone after his wife and son . . . he would have been admitting he needed them and that would have reflected weakness."

"But maybe he *did* need them!" the old man exclaimed.

"Yeah, I expect he did," Longarm said. "In fact, he told me years later that he should have quit his job and gone after his wife and son. It was, he said, the biggest mistake of his life."

"Can you find his wife and son?"

"I'll do my best."

"But first you want to find out who shot your friend, huh?"

"That's right. I just hope Monty is still alive so I can see and talk to him one last time, and he can tell me who he thinks shot him from ambush."

"When are you leaving for Arizona?"

"When is the first westbound train out of town?"

Oliver retrieved his pocket watch and said, "There's one leaving in exactly two hours and ten minutes."

"I'll be on it."

"Don't worry about your place. I'll watch out for your

4

stuff, collect your mail and do whatever you need done."

Longarm pushed himself out of his rocking chair. "I'd better go see my boss at his house. Billy Vail won't be happy about me leaving, but it's something that I have to do."

"What about Miss Rosie? She'll be coming around soon enough."

"Yeah." Longarm removed the unlit cigar from his mouth and shoved it back into his coat pocket. "Will you tell her that I had to go to Arizona and why?"

"Sure," Oliver said, "but you know she'll get upset."

"She'll cry and carry on, but she'll get over it." Longarm allowed himself a dry smile. "Rosie won't be twenty-four hours without a boyfriend. She'll have a new one before tomorrow night."

"Ahh," Oliver said, blushing a little because he was basically a very shy and modest old gent. "I wouldn't say that."

"I know Rosie, and you don't. She won't pine for me long, I can assure you."

"Don't matter," Oliver said. "You get women as quick and easy as a dog catches ticks and fleas."

Longarm actually managed a smile. "Thanks for your help, Oliver. I'll try and be back within two weeks."

"Not a chance," the hotel owner said. "First you got to find and catch your friend's killer. Then you got to find his wife . . . a woman that I gather he hasn't seen in how many years?"

"About eleven or twelve."

"Not an easy thing to do."

"Henrietta used to be quite a looker," Longarm said. "A woman that men noticed and remembered. If she hasn't lost her looks, I expect I'll soon cross someone who remembers her and the boy."

"What if she doesn't even have the kid anymore. What did you say his name was?"

"Tyler."

5

"Well," Oliver said, "she might have ran off and left him just like she left your friend."

Longarm hadn't even considered that possibility. But he did remember that Henrietta liked nice things and sweet talking gamblers with money. It was, he supposed, entirely possible that the woman had abandoned Tyler Kilpatrick. As hard as it was to believe, some women had no love for motherhood. Longarm had seen them way too often, and it was always pretty heartbreaking to see what that did to a young child. But Tyler would be twelve now . . . possibly even thirteen. He was a young fella soon to be a grown man.

"I wonder if Tyler even knows who his real father was," Longarm mused aloud.

Oliver nodded his head. "I was just asking myself that very same question."

Longarm went back to his room and packed his traveling bag complete with a change of clothes and his shaving gear. As he was about to leave and go to see Billy Vail, it occurred to him that this trip was personal business and that meant he would have to pay all his own expenses.

For a moment, Longarm stood with his hand poised over his doorknob, trying to imagine what it would cost him to find Monty's ambusher and his long lost wife and son. The round-trip train fare alone would be sixty or seventy dollars, then he'd have to rent a horse or maybe ride stagecoaches in his search for the woman and her son. Even if he scrimped, which was not his nature, he quickly calculated that this trip might well cost him a couple hundred dollars.

He didn't have a couple hundred dollars in cash. Longarm dragged out his wallet and counted forty-three dollars. He had a couple hundred more in his bank account but the bank was closed until Monday morning at nine o'clock.

I can't wait here until the bank opens! Monty is dying. What am I going to do?

Rosie wasn't good for the money . . . she was always broke. That left only his boss, Billy Vail. Longarm knew that Billy, despite having a wife and children, was in good financial shape and that he squirreled away cash at his home in addition to having a hefty savings account at the bank.

Longarm sighed. Not only would he have to ask Billy for permission to take an emergency leave of absence . . . but he'd have to ask him for a cash advance against his salary. It was going to be tough. Billy wasn't one to let go of a dollar easily, not even to a friend in need.

"Well," Longarm muttered, "he's my only hope."

It took Longarm fifteen minutes to reach the tree-lined residential neighborhood located just to the west of Cherry Creek. Billy Vail lived in a sturdy brick house with a lawn and a garden and some flower boxes filled with red blossoms. Longarm knew that Billy's wife had a green thumb and could make anything grow.

He knocked on the door, checked his watch and saw that his train would be pulling out in one hour. Billy opened the door. After an initial expression of surprise, he smiled. "Well, Custis, what brings you around late on a Saturday afternoon?"

"I've got an emergency," Longarm said. "Do you remember my old friend, Monty Kilpatrick?"

"Of course. Come on inside."

But Longarm hesitated. "I'd rather just tell you what's happened right out here on the porch."

Billy closed the door and led Longarm to a chair. "Have a seat. You don't look too good."

Longarm retrieved the letter from the inside of his coat pocket and handed it wordlessly to Billy.

"You want me to read this?"

"It explains everything quicker than I could."

"All right." Billy read the letter, his expression darkening. He shook his head, then read the letter a second time before folding it up and handing it to Longarm. "So when are you leaving?"

"In an hour."

Billy muttered something under his breath. "I was going to send you to Montana on Monday. There's some big trouble up there that I felt you were best qualified to handle."

"You're going to have to send someone else," Longarm insisted. "I can't just ignore this letter."

"But the man might well already be dead."

"That doesn't change the fact that he's asked me to deliver his personal things to his son and to tell the boy about his father. Billy, you know that I have to do this."

"Yeah," the marshal said. "All right. Catch your train."

"I . . . I . . ."

"Let me guess," Billy said quietly. "You need traveling money."

"Yeah."

"How much?"

"A couple of hundred ought to do it if I watch my expenses closely."

"That's probably all you have saved in the world."

Longarm said nothing.

"Look," Billy said, scratching his head and thinking hard. "There's some trouble in Arizona that I've been needing to have one of my people look into."

"What kind of trouble?"

"A federal officer . . . Deputy Marshal Boone is his name . . . has been accused of abusing his office and extorting money from the merchants in a town called Paradise."

"Is that anywhere near Mountain City?"

"I have no idea, but it's bound to be a lot closer than it is to Denver. So why don't you make it a point to go to Paradise and look into this problem with Marshal Boone? If he's abusing his office and extorting money, then we need to get rid of him. If he's not . . . well, we need to find what axes his accusers have to grind. It could

8

be that Boone is simply doing his job and has crossed some important people. At any rate, I need to find out the truth and then see what can be done. One bad apple can ruin the whole barrel, if you see what I mean."

"I see what you mean."

Billy clapped Longarm on the shoulder. "If you go to Paradise and handle this business, we can write off your travel expenses and that way you don't have to wipe out your meager savings."

"That would be greatly appreciated," Longarm said. "But I have to take care of Monty's business first."

"I understand completely. But just make sure you also take care of *our* business before you return to the office."

"Yes, sir."

"Custis, I know that Monty saved your life, and I know how much you admired him."

"He was one of the finest lawmen I ever met. Before he was transferred to the Arizona Territory from here, we were close friends. I learned almost as much from Monty as I learned from you."

Billy managed a half-smile. "You're nice to say that. And I wish you the very best in Arizona. If you run out of funds or need any help . . . don't hesitate to send a tele-gram."

"It might take up to a month to handle this."

"Then you will definitely need more cash. Just wire us as usual, and we'll send it along. But you have to take care of the federal business or else I'll have to ask for a reimbursement."

"I understand, and I will see what is going on with Marshal Boone."

"Yes, do that. As you probably remember, he was a tough hombre and he had a short fuse, so be careful. If he is guilty and suspects that you've been sent to inves-tigate, he could be dangerous."

"I'm aware of that fact."

Billy stuck out his hand. "Good luck, Custis. I sure

9

wish I could have sent you to Montana, but I guess I'll have to send John Woolsey."

"He'll do fine. He's a good man."

"Yeah, but he's green, and he doesn't have your contacts."

"He'll do fine," Longarm repeated.

"You got time for a drink while I get you the cash?"

"Not really. Train leaves in . . ." Longarm consulted his watch. "Forty minutes."

"Then I'll be right back."

Billy disappeared but returned very quickly with the cash. "There's two hundred and twenty-five dollars and more if you need it."

"Thanks."

As Longarm was about to turn and leave, Billy said, "I sure don't envy you this trip. Just find them."

"You mean the man that ambushed Monty?"

"Yes, and his son, Tyler. Tell him I said that his father was a fine lawman and a credit to himself and his government. Tell the kid that his old man was one of the very best."

"I will."

Longarm shoved Billy's money deep in his pockets and headed for the train.

Chapter 2

It took Longarm nearly a week to reach the little ranching and timber settlement of Mountain City in Northern Arizona. The town was located just a few miles south of Flagstaff in some of the prettiest mountain country west of the Rockies. Longarm hadn't been to this part of the country for almost two years, and when he stepped off the stagecoach and gathered his bags, he surveyed the bustling town and said, "This place has grown considerable in the last year."

"Yep," the stagecoach driver replied, spitting a thick brown stream of tobacco onto the rump of his wheel horse. "I expect we've got almost a thousand people living here right now. Couple of big logging companies are putting out a good-sized payroll and cattle prices are holding strong. If we could get more water, I expect that there'd been some farmin', although the growin' season is short. We got three outfits raisin' sheep but they ain't too popular among the cowboys."

"Nothing wrong with sheep."

"Nope, long as they're cooked and simmerin' hot on your plate."

The man spat again, and Longarm frowned wondering why he felt compelled to spit on the back of his wheel horse which was a dapple gray and by far the man's best looking horse. "Mister," Longarm finally blurted, "how come you do that?"

"What?"

"Spit on that fine looking dapple gray."

"Well, sir," the driver said, working up a quick spit and pasting the gray once more, "the sad truth of it is that that damned horse is so pretty that he has taken a big shine to hisself and sometimes he needs to be taken down a peg or two or else he'll get obstreperous."

Longarm shook his head. "You really think that horse knows how bad your tobacco spit looks on him?"

"Sure he does! And so does his three partners. Once I unhitch that team and turn 'em out in the corral, the gray will be so mortified he'll stand alone in a corner so's he can't see or hear the others makin' fun of him. Then, he'll be a whole lot easier to work for the next couple of weeks."

Longarm wasn't an expert on horses and had trouble believing the coachman. But since it wasn't worth arguing about, he gathered his traveling bag and said, "I'm looking for Marshal Kilpatrick."

"Cemetery is right up the hill," the driver said, his smile dying. "Marshal Monty died only two days ago."

"Damn," Longarm whispered, his hands clenching at his sides in helpless frustration.

"Stranger, are you his friend . . . or a creditor?"

"I was his friend."

"A lawman?"

Normally, Longarm did not reveal his purpose or even the fact that he was a lawman until it best served his purposes. But now, he just nodded his head. "Yes, I'm a federal deputy marshal, and I've come to pay my respects and to find out who shot Monty."

"Good luck," the driver said, looking morose. "Nobody around here knows who would do such a thing. The marshal was well liked and respected. I'm not saying he didn't have enemies. You couldn't do the job unless you broke a few heads, arrested a few that needed arresting and even sent the worst of 'em to jail or the gallows. But everyone knew the rules in this town and understood that our marshal never played favorites. He did his job and was fair to us all."

"That's exactly what I would have expected."

"You come to take his place?" The driver spat another big, goopy stream and this time it struck the gray on his front shoulder and ran down like thick maple syrup.

"Nope. I just came to see him and to find out who killed Monty and why."

"Well, Marshal, when you do find out who ambushed our Kilpatrick, you're gonna have your hands full keeping him alive because everyone in Mountain City will want to string him up by the neck."

"Is there a circuit judge serving this town?"

"Nope. But Judge Lawson comes up from Flagstaff whenever he's needed. He's a good man, and he don't mind hanging the guilty."

"Okay," Longarm said. "Point me in the direction of the cemetery."

Ten minutes later, Longarm dropped his travel bag and squatted on his heels beside the freshly dug grave. Someone had erected a simple wooden cross and on it painted these words:

MARSHAL MONTY KILPATRICK WAS A DAMNED GOOD
LAWMAN WHO WILL BE SORELY MISSED

Longarm felt a big, painful knot fill his throat. Monty had been the one who'd taken Custis under his wing when he was young and green behind the ears. He'd taught him how to be a better judge of men . . . those good and bad . . . and how to keep from getting himself killed while he was learning the ropes. Even so, when Longarm had made a bad mistake and a prisoner had pulled a hidden derringer from his boot-top determined to send Custis to an early

13

grave, it had been Monty who'd dove between them, taking the bullet across his own ribs.

Longarm took off his flat brimmed hat and ran his fingers across the dark earth of the grave. "Monty, you laid there cussin' and bleedin' while I finally handcuffed that prisoner, and you told me through clenched teeth that I'd been far too trusting. You said to always search a prisoner, and then get his hands locked behind his back before I did anything else. I never forgot that advice, and it has served me well. Wasn't until we got to the doctor that we learned the bullet had broken four of your ribs."

A stiffening breeze whispered through the tall pines, and Longarm looked up to see the approach of an afternoon storm. It would rain, and he recalled that Monty had always enjoyed the afternoon high mountain showers that this country received in August. But Monty wasn't able to enjoy them anymore, thanks to someone who probably thought they were going to get away with murder.

"I'll find out who did this to you, and I'll see that he pays full measure," Longarm vowed with a quaver in his voice. "I hope you knew for sure that I was coming, and that I'll set things right, just for you, my friend."

Longarm shook his head and came to his feet. He replaced his hat on his head, absently brushed the gun on his left hip and whispered, "And after I find your boy, I'll see that you get a proper headstone. One that will last a hundred years or more so that Tyler . . . and his sons and daughters . . . can find this resting place, if they ever have a notion."

He turned and left the cemetery, his pace quickening as he walked downhill and back into Mountain City. Since Monty had been the only law in the town, Longarm headed for his office to see if the mayor or city council had found a replacement. But when he got to the little office with its single cell, the place was locked and a sign tacked to the door said that if anyone had trouble, they should visit Mayor Abe Townsend who ran Townsend's Dry Goods Store.

Entering the store a few minutes later, Longarm saw a tall, skinny man in his mid-fifties wearing a black suit and white shirt standing behind the counter passing the time of day with a young woman. The woman was plump but quite pretty with light brown hair and an hourglass figure. Longarm pretended to look at some canned goods but that soon wore thin so he stepped up to the pair and said, "Excuse me. Are you Mayor Abe Townsend?"

Townsend managed a smile that lacked any real warmth. "I am. What can I do for you?"

Longarm extending his hand. "I'm Deputy Marshal Custis Long from Denver. Monty Kilpatrick and I were old friends, and I've come here as fast as I could to see what I could do to help."

Townsend's smile evaporated but his grip was firm as he said, "I'm afraid you're a little too late to be of any help. Monty is dead and buried."

"I know. I was just up to the cemetery. Are you planning to buy him a proper headstone?"

"It's been ordered," the store owner and mayor said. "We took a collection and raised nearly a hundred dollars. It will be a fine, impressive marble headstone and it should arrive next week."

"Glad to hear that," Longarm said. He turned to the young woman and said, "Sorry to have interrupted your conversation."

"That's quite all right. I'm Rita Townsend, and this is my stepfather. We were very fond of Marshal Kilpatrick. I'm just sorry that you've come all this way in vain."

"Oh but I haven't," Longarm said. "Unless Monty's ambusher has been found and sentenced."

"He hasn't," the mayor said. "Although there are some obvious suspects, no one has any real idea who shot our marshal."

"Then I'll start off with a list of your 'obvious suspects' and go from there."

"Of course," the man said. "Have you been assigned to take Marshal Kilpatrick's place until the murder is solved?"

"No. I'm with the federal government. Monty used to work for us but he left the agency many years ago."

"That's too bad," the mayor said. "I haven't talked to the town council but we're going to need someone to replace Marshal Kilpatrick."

"That's right," Longarm said. "Until then, I'll be around for a while."

"You mean," Rita Townsend said, "until you either find out who ambushed Marshal Kilpatrick or give up the search?"

"I won't give up," Longarm vowed with more than a little passion. "Monty saved my life once, and I owe it to him to make the arrest. He also sent me a letter requesting that his personal belongings and whatever he had in the bank be delivered to his son."

"Yes," the young woman said, "we all knew that he had a boy that would be about thirteen now."

"Any idea where I can locate Tyler and his mother?"

"I'm afraid not," Rita said, looking at her stepfather who also shook his head. "But I do know that Henrietta died about five years ago."

Longarm blinked with surprise. "Then what happened to Tyler?"

"I really can't say."

"Where and why did Henrietta die?"

"Monty heard that she passed away from a fever in some awful little town along the Colorado River. He went to claim his son but never found the boy. Someone told him that Tyler went to California with Henrietta's sister. But no one knew if that was true or not."

Longarm scowled. "It would seem that I'm going to have a hard time finding either Monty's killer or his son."

"I'm afraid that might be true," the mayor said.

"What I'll need," Longarm told them both, "is a list of anyone you think might have had it in for your marshal."

"Mister," Townsend said, "over the years, Monty arrested a lot of people and made a considerable number of enemies."

16

"Along with a great many friends and admirers of which you can count myself and my father," Rita quickly added.

"We loved the man," Townsend said, misery rising up in his eyes. "The folks in Flagstaff and Prescott kept trying to hire him away from us, but Monty loved Mountain City and thought of it as his permanent home. He'd often tell us that he planned to retire here, and he'd built a nice cabin just outside of town on about forty acres."

"How far out of town?"

"Not more than a mile."

"Then that's where I'll be staying while I conduct the search for his killer," Longarm said, deciding to save himself and the government some hotel lodging money. "Now how about a written list of who might have had it in for Monty."

"Can you give us an hour?" Rita asked.

Longarm wasn't pleased with the delay, but he guessed that since Monty had been shot almost two weeks previously, another hour wouldn't matter. "All right. The important thing is that you take your time and put everyone on the list who might have hated Monty enough to put a bullet in his gut. And I'll want to know where to find them."

"Some moved away or are still in prison."

"Then don't put their names down unless they still live within a hundred miles of here," Longarm decided. "I'll start with the ones living closest who hated Monty the most."

"That would be the cattle ranchers," Rita said without a moment's hesitation. "They opposed Marshal Kilpatrick and accused him of favoring the sheep men. But he didn't. He just tried to keep the peace in this country and that was never easy. Cattlemen just naturally seem to hate sheep men."

"So I've noticed," Longarm said. "So who is the biggest cattle rancher in these parts?

"Wade Black. He owns the Rocking J Ranch that runs all the way to the south rim of the Grand Canyon. Must run five or six thousand head of cattle."

"Put him at the top of the list."

"You won't find him easy to deal with."

Longarm shrugged. "Miss Townsend, I am not here to make friends. I'm here for one reason only and that is to find my friend's murderer."

"Do you have a horse?" Townsend asked. "Because you'll need one to get out to the Rocking J."

"Where can I rent one?"

"You don't have to do that," Rita said. "I've got a couple of good saddle horses that rarely get exercised. I'll loan you my roan gelding. He's a handful but he's strong and surefooted. Maybe you can ride him down for me."

"Maybe," Longarm agreed, "because I might have to ride some long trails in a hurry. I could even lame him."

"If you ruin the animal, you'll owe me sixty dollars, which is what I paid for him," she said. "But I'm not too worried. You look like a responsible man."

"I am."

"Why don't you two go get the horse while I work up a list of suspects?" Townsend offered.

Longarm thought that was a good idea. "I'll be back soon."

"Rita," the mayor said, "I'm going to close up here for a few minutes when I've finished the list and talk to a couple of my friends just in case they have a name or two to add that I've forgotten."

"And I'll also want to look the list over," she said, heading for the door.

Longarm thanked the mayor and followed his step-daughter outside. She had a pretty nice swing to her ca-boose and, under more pleasant circumstances, he would have liked to have examined the source of those provoc-atively swaying hips. But these weren't pleasant circum-stances and, until he caught Monty's killer, he would keep to his own grim business.

18

"I own a house just up the street, but I keep my horses at the livery."

"Then let's go see that roan gelding. You've got a saddle, bridle and everything I need?"

"Sure do. Are you a good rider?"

"I'm no bronc buster, but I get by," he said, wondering how spirited the roan gelding really might be. "And, if your horse is unreliable, I'd just as soon pass on him."

"Roanie is no outlaw," she said as they headed for the livery. "He's sound and he might look a little fat, but he's solid. He has good feet and, when he gallops, he won't drive your head into your spine. He's easy gaited and a handsome devil, but he can be mighty rambunctious when you first saddle him."

"I can deal with that."

"I expect you can deal with almost anything," she said, her eyes moving up and down his tall, solidly built body. "You married?"

"Nope."

"Why not?"

"Never quite got lucky enough, I guess."

"Luck runs hot and cold. Maybe you just haven't found the right woman."

"Maybe."

She looked right into his eyes and smiled. "Why don't you come by my house tonight, and I'll cook you a good meal?"

"I, uh . . ."

"And I'll tell you what I know about the people on the list that Father is preparing. It'll take awhile."

Longarm thought he had nothing to lose, and everything to gain, by taking her offer even though he was not in the mood for romance and wanted to keep his entire focus on the murder investigation.

"All right."

"Good," she said brightly. "I'll cook you some chicken and dumplings and an apple pie."

"Don't go to too much bother."

"No bother. As you can tell by looking at me, I love to eat."

"So do I."

"Yes, but you're slender, and I'm not."

"Only in the right places," he said without thinking while his eyes were irresistibly drawn to her ample bosom.

Rita Townsend blushed and then they went into the livery to see "Rambunctious" Roanie.

Chapter 3

As they approached the livery, Rita lowered her voice and said, "Just don't let Ivan get your goat."

"Who's Ivan?"

"He owns the livery and . . . well, he *thinks* he owns me. But he doesn't. We were engaged to be married last year but then I came to my senses and called it off."

Longarm shrugged. "I've always felt that it is far better to be single than to be locked into a bad marriage."

"That's what my stepfather said and so did a lot of other people that I trust. But I wanted to warn you that Ivan can be rough and intimidating. He's run a lot of good men away from me."

"I can handle him. Besides, all I want is the loan of your horse and saddle."

"Roanie hasn't been ridden in quite a while. Ivan used to ride him at least once a week to keep him from getting too rambunctious, but since I broke up with the man, I don't think the horse hardly ever gets ridden."

"Why don't you just sell him?"

"I'm thinking about it, and I guess I would . . . if I could find a buyer. In fact I'd let him go for fifty dollars." She looked up at Longarm, and there was no doubt she was offering him the horse for sale.

Longarm frowned thinking that Roanie must have earned a bad reputation, and that's why he was unsalable.

"Ivan!" she called as they stood in front of the dim interior of the rickety old barn. "Are you in there?"

"Yeah!" came an answering roar.

"Well, come on out. I want you to meet a friend that I'm going to let borrow Roanie."

"Why don't we just go in there and get your saddle, bridle and blanket?" Longarm asked. "I can carry them around to wherever the horse is and saddle him. We don't need to bother the man."

"Oh," Rita said, "Ivan isn't so busy, and he wouldn't want us in there without him being close. Ivan is kind of . . . well, territorial. He doesn't let anyone on his property unless he knows and likes them."

"I'm comin'," a low voice growled. "Just restin' up a bit. What you want to go loan your horse to someone else for?"

"He needs a good, sound horse to ride."

Just then, one of the biggest men that Longarm had met in quite some time emerged from the dark interior of the livery barn. He was barefooted and bare chested and he looked as if he was part grizzly bear with a full beard and a thick mat of black hair covering his massive torso.

"Who the hell is this?" Ivan snarled when he stepped up to Longarm while adjusting his suspenders.

"I'm Deputy United States Marshal Long," Custis said, extending his hand and trying to keep from wrinkling his nose at the stench of the filthy giant.

Ivan's huge hand wrapped around Longarm's and tried to crush it in a grip so powerful that it was all Longarm could do to keep from stomping the liveryman's bare toes or else smashing him in his hairy face with his left hand. Longarm was a big man and plenty strong, but he knew that he could not begin to match Ivan's brute power.

"Ivan, let go of him! If you break his hand like you did Pete's last year . . . why, I'll never speak to you again!"

The giant finally released Longarm's hand which felt as if it had been stepped on by a two thousand pound shod draft horse. Trying hard not to grimace, Custis stuck his hand behind his back and silently worked his fingers, testing them to see if their bones were broken. He guessed they weren't, but that didn't make him feel any better toward Ivan, who was looking very pleased with himself.

"What the hell are you doin' in Mountain City?" he rumbled, folding his massive arms across his chest and glaring down from a height of at least six foot six.

"I came to pay my respects to Monty Kilpatrick. He was an old friend who wrote me a deathbed letter."

"He was a lawman, and I never met one that was much worth looking up to."

"Monty was worth looking up to . . . even by someone as big as yourself," Longarm shot back, wanting to smash the giant in his nose and see if he could break it with one perfect overhand punch.

Ivan chose that moment to noisily pass wind in order to show that he did not share Longarm's opinion of Kilpatrick.

"We need to get my saddle and tack so that Custis here can get Roanie. He's going to be staying at Marshal Kilpatrick's place until he finds out who killed him."

"I'll get your horse saddled and bridled," Ivan grunted.

"Don't trouble yourself," Longarm said. "I can do it myself."

Ivan's thick lips turned with contempt. "You don't know Roanie like I do. Just stay right here, and I'll do it my way."

"Suit yourself."

Ivan disappeared into his barn, and when Longarm turned to Rita, she just shrugged. "I told you he was rough."

"He's more than rough," Longarm said, still working the pain out of his fingers. "Ivan is pure mean. You were right not to marry that man. Has he ever killed anyone?"

"Probably. The thing is, he's so big and strong that very

23

few men would even try to fight him unless they were close to his size or else very drunk."

"He needs a serious lesson in manners," Longarm said.

Rita nodded. "And you think maybe you're man enough to give it to him?"

"I'm man enough," Longarm replied. "I could have stomped his toes with the heel of my boot and broken them the way he just tried to break my fingers. But then I'd have had to also either shoot or pistol-whip the man, and I didn't want it to go that far."

"Do you really think you could have whipped him down to size?" she asked, eyes bright with interest... even excitement.

"Look, I'm here to find out who killed my friend and not to prove how much of a man I am. And, to be honest, taking on 'Ivan the Terrible' could get me hurt, and I need to be able to do my job. So let's just get your horse and see if Roanie and I can get along in peace and harmony. If he bucks then I'll want some other animal. I haven't the time or the interest to teach your horse... or Ivan... their manners."

"Well," she said, clearly disappointed that Longarm wasn't going to show his stuff, "I hope Roanie behaves today."

"Me, too. And I'll tell you something else. Ivan still thinks that you're his girl, and I'm not sure that anything is going to change his mind."

"Monty was the only one that ever stood up to Ivan," she said, biting her lip in an obvious attempt to fight back tears. "He told Ivan that he'd shoot him dead if he got crazy and tried to whip him."

"Did Ivan want to fight Monty?"

"Sure! I was sweet on Monty. I always invited him over for Sunday supper, and he knew where he could come if he got cold at night."

Longarm had to smile. "So you and Monty were... were pretty close, huh?"

"We often slept together. I think he'd have eventually

caved in and married me. I knew that he still carried a torch for that damned old Henrietta, though I could never figure out why. But when Monty got a little tight on rye whiskey, he'd sometimes talk about that bitch . . . only he never called her that word. He said it was his fault that she left him with their son. And when I asked him what he did that was so terrible, he said that he couldn't give up being a lawman and she wanted him to be a whole lot more."

Longarm looked quickly away, fighting back bitterness. "I didn't know that."

"I'll have to say this much . . . Henrietta Kilpatrick was a real looker. I was only a kid the first time that I saw her, but I remember thinking that she was one of the prettiest women I ever laid my eyes upon. But she was cold as ice, and she had a bad reputation. If you ask me, she never wanted to have children."

"Well," Longarm said, "Henrietta is dead now, and there's no good comes to anyone from talking bad about the dead."

"Sure, Custis, but I thought you might want to know about her and then Monty and me. My own mother died when I was young, so I can imagine what Tyler must feel like right now. But my stepfather is a good man, and he takes care of me. I work for him when I feel like it, and he gave me the house I live in so I could be independent."

"He sounds like a fine man."

"He is," Rita said. "He and Monty got along real good and said that our age difference shouldn't matter. That Monty would make me a good husband."

"How old are you?"

She smiled. "I'm twenty-four now."

"You are young," Longarm said, surprised because he'd gauged her to be about ten years older.

"In a small town, a twenty-four-year-old unmarried woman is considered to be in full bloom, soon to be a faded rose."

"That's ridiculous."

25

"Maybe, but that's what people say. And I could have gotten married lots of times . . . except for Ivan."

"Your father is the town mayor. Can't he do something about that man?"

"What do you suggest?"

Longarm toed the soft earth and listened to the approaching rumble of thunder. "I don't know. Buy the man out on the condition that Ivan leaves Mountain City?"

"Ivan wouldn't sell. He's got everything he wants in that smelly old barn, and he *is* good with horses. He's also the town's blacksmith, and there's none better. He does better than you'd imagine."

"Given his attitude and personality, that's hard to believe."

"Oh, he's not so bad except when he thinks I might be interested in another man. That's why he crushed Pete's hand and sent him packin'. Monty was the only one that Ivan respected and let me see, although he wasn't a bit happy about that. Oh, here he comes now with Roanie."

Longarm took the roan gelding in at a glance and judged him to be a very handsome horse. Like Rita had warned, the animal was on the heavy side, maybe carrying as much as two hundred extra pounds of fat. But he was tall, straight-legged with a good conformation and a quick, reasonably intelligent look about him that Longarm appreciated.

"Nice looking horse, isn't he?" Rita said a little proudly.

"Yes, he is."

"I fell in love the first time I saw him buck off a cowboy down in front of the Bent Fork Saloon."

"Bucked him off?"

"Yeah, but he was drunk and raising Cain. Shooting his gun off and racing Roanie up and down the street. I admired the horse for bucking the cowboy off. Threw him right into a water trough and then Marshal Monty arrested him before he could drown."

"Is that a fact?"

26

"Yep."

"Here's the horse," Ivan rumbled. "Good luck if you think you can ride him, lawman."

"Ivan, don't you say that. Roanie just needs a little more exercise and a good hand at his reins."

"Sure does," Ivan said with a smirk on his fat lips. "That's why I'm the only one that he trusts and who can ride him."

Longarm ignored the insult. He walked all around the horse, then placed his hand on the blaze between Roanie's eyes. He scratched the gelding's forehead and then worked his way up between the geldings ears. The animal leaned in a little and that meant he was enjoying being scratched.

"He seems to be good-hearted."

"He is," Rita said. "You can see why I bought him."

"Five dollars says he'll pitch you in the dirt," Ivan hissed.

Longarm was no cowboy, and he didn't want to waste Billy Vail's money or his own, but he couldn't ignore the challenge. "You're on."

Ivan grinned showing big horse teeth. He reached into his pockets and found a wad of crumpled bills. Counting them out, he handed them to Rita saying, "Get his money, too."

Longarm gave Rita five dollars. "Are you sure he isn't a bucker?"

"Not if you go real slow and let him get used to you in the saddle before you try to gallop."

"I believe you," Longarm said, checking the cinch because he didn't trust Ivan farther than he could throw him.

The cinch was tight and everything looked fine except that the stirrups were a bit too long. "I'll adjust the stirrups before I get on."

"Don't waste our time," Ivan said. "They're fine for you."

But Longarm ignored the man and after carefully adjusting them to his own leg length, he figured that he was ready to climb on board and see what Roanie was all about.

"Here we go," he said.

"Just don't jerk the bit up in his mouth," Rita warned, backing away with worry in her eyes. "Take it slow at first."

Longarm jammed his left boot into the stirrup and swung up into the saddle. But Roanie exploded before he could get his right foot into the stirrup or become well seated.

It was no contest. Three jolting jumps from the powerful gelding and Longarm was airborne. He landed hard, bruising his left shoulder on the packed earth and hearing Ivan's braying laughter.

"Marshal!" Rita cried, hurrying up to his side. "Are you hurt?"

Longarm was hurt, but not badly. Mostly, he was angry at being ridiculed by the giant and losing five dollars. He glared at Ivan as the liveryman cornered the roan gelding between a chicken pen and a corral and then grabbed the gelding's reins. Ivan had Roanie under immediate control, and Longarm would have simply let the matter end, despite his wounded pride, but he saw the giant reach back under the saddle blanket near Roanie's rump and remove something.

"Hey!" Longarm shouted, jumping to his feet and rushing over to the man and horse. "What did you put under his saddle blanket that made him buck so hard?"

"What the hell are you talking about!" Ivan demanded, stepping away from the gelding and acting confused.

Longarm could see that Ivan had something clenched in his massive fist, and the only way he was going to get a good look at it was to do what he'd wanted to do right from the start and that was to stomp Ivan's bare toes with the solid heel of his boot.

He did a good job of it, too! Probably broke all four toes an instant before he shoved the giant over backward, causing him to land in the dirt and involuntarily release the wicked looking ball of barbed wire that had been hidden in his fist.

Longarm snatched up the small but vicious irritant and showed it to Rita. "See what he did to your horse?"

"Ivan!" she stormed. "How could you do that?"

The giant didn't answer but came to his feet. His face was twisted with pain, but his eyes were as mean as the twin barrels of a loaded shotgun. And despite his broken toes, he threw himself at Longarm with a demented fury.

Custis was expecting a rush, and he anticipated that, like most muscle-bound men, Ivan would be slow. He was right and it was easy enough to step aside as the liveryman lumbered past. Longarm did not waste the opportunity to smash Ivan in the side of his ponderous jaw, knocking him back to the ground.

"I'm going to kill you," the giant said, crawling to his bare feet and trying to keep his weight off his broken toes.

"Then get busy at it," Longarm said, rolling his bruised shoulder and raising his fists.

Ivan came at him feigning a right cross and hurling dirt from his left hand into Longarm's eyes. Momentarily blinded, Longarm tried to fend off the bigger man's furious attack, but Ivan's blows struck his upraised arms like cannonballs knocking down a flimsy fortress wall. Breaking through Longarm's guard, a single blow to the side of his jaw sent him reeling into the chicken pen, knocking it over and causing a flock of hens to get hysterical with their squawking and screeching.

Ivan was on Longarm like an avalanche, and while he tried to clear his vision, he got tangled up in the chicken wire and broken wood fencing. The giant began pounding his body. Longarm knew that he was finished. He couldn't get out from under the huge man's weight, and he still couldn't see clearly.

The sound of a gunshot exploded almost in their faces and Rita shouted, "Ivan, get off him or I swear that I'll put a bullet in your stupid brain right *now*!"

To emphasize the point, Rita Townsend fired again, and

Longarm swore that he felt the heat of the slug pass inches from his face. Ivan's immense bulk lifted and the man hissed, "Next time I will kill you, lawman!"

Custis scrubbed a forearm across his eyes, finally clearing them, and as Ivan started to turn toward Rita, he kicked upward with all his strength, sending his boot directly between Ivan's tree-trunk-sized legs.

The giant bellowed in pain, and Longarm bounced to his feet and went at him with both fists just as hard as he could swing. Every blow Longarm landed sent Ivan reeling backward until the giant slammed up against the side of his barn and covered his bloody face with his hands.

"I ought to arrest you, but you're not worth the time or effort," Longarm said. "But if you ever try a stunt like you did with me and that horse . . . then I'll break not only your toes but your fingers and your damned neck! Do you understand me?"

Ivan's hands were still covering his bearded and bloodied face, but Longarm could see his eyes between his fingers, and he'd never seen anyone with such hatred.

"Rita, let's go," Longarm ordered, feeling as though he'd been thrown down one of Virginia City, Nevada's thousand-foot mine shafts.

"What about Roanie?"

Longarm went over and gathered the horse's reins. "I'll buy him," he replied, digging for his wallet and finding the money.

"But he bucked you off!" she said while taking his money.

"Only because of that barbed wire under his blanket. Let's go!"

Longarm was feeling so bad that he didn't want to ride out to Monty Kilpatrick's old place so he allowed Rita to lead him to her little house at the end of Grant Avenue.

"I'll take Roanie and put him in the back yard," she said. "And tomorrow, I'll get my other horse and find another place to board her."

"Fine with me," Longarm said. "I need to rinse all the dirt out of my eyes."

"Come on inside. You also look like you could use a drink."

"I sure could, and I don't mean water."

"I'll make you a wonderful supper, and you can get out of those clothes and I'll wash them for you."

"That's not necessary."

She tied Roanie to her fence, then put her arm around his waist and helped him up her front porch and inside. "Take a seat and relax while I get you a washcloth and basin of cool water to bathe your face and hands."

"Bring the whiskey first, and then take care of your horse. I'll be better when you return."

When Longarm had a glass in his fist and the first evidence of a warm glow in his gut, he sat back and surveyed Rita's cozy parlor. It was nice with lots of books and good, solid furniture that looked as if it should have belonged in a man's library. Maybe it had belonged to Mr. Townsend, and he'd given it to Rita.

Longarm's clothes were soiled not only with dirt, but with chicken shit. What a stinking mess! But if Rita helped him with the clothes, he guessed he could right the wrong inflicted upon him by that damned Ivan. Longarm clenched and unclenched his fists. His knuckles were all bruised and cut and his right eye was swollen half shut.

"Damn!" he muttered out loud. "This is one hell of a sorry way to start things off in Arizona. First, I don't reach town until after Monty passes on . . . then, I'm nearly killed by a horse and a demented and jealous liveryman who could pass for a grizzly bear."

Longarm ran his battered fingers through his hair and took liberties with the liquor, because it was excellent stuff, and because he was in a world of pain and smelled like a pig who had rolled in a chicken pen.

Chapter 4

"You sure are a mess," Rita said, coming in from the back yard through her kitchen to stand in the parlor doorway. "How are you feeling?"

"I'll live," he said. "Got any ice?"

"As a matter of fact I do," she said. "I'll go down to the cellar and cut you off a chunk, so you can try to hold that swelling down enough to see out of that eye. You sure got popped!"

"Yeah."

She came over and took the glass of whiskey from Longarm's hand, then took several swallows before raising the glass and proclaiming, "Here's to you, Marshal Custis Long! I never thought I'd live to see the day when someone whipped Ivan. But you did it, and I'm just proud to have witnessed such an amazing feat!"

Longarm couldn't help but smile at her excitement. "Well," he said, "I whipped him all right but it took some doing. If I hadn't of kicked him where a man is most vulnerable, I'm not sure I'd be conscious or maybe even alive right now."

"I think you're right," she said, nodding her head and then handing him back his glass. "Once you caught him in the balls, the starch ran right out of him. If you'd have

33

missed . . . well, I'd have probably had to shoot Ivan to save your life."

"You'd have done that?"

"You bet I would have." She bent over and gave him a kiss on the forehead, then wrinkled her nose and said, "Phew! You sure do stink! I'll start a bath for you and get that ice."

"Be much appreciated," he said. "And I wonder if you can really get my clothes cleaned by tomorrow morning."

"I doubt it, but I'll send them down to Yo Fat, our Chinese laundry man first thing tomorrow morning. He'll have them back to you by this time tomorrow just as fresh as flowers."

"Then what am I supposed to wear tomorrow when I go out to see Wade Black at his Rocking J Ranch?"

"I've got some clothes that might fit you."

"Whose?" Longarm asked suspiciously.

"Well, Monty was about your size."

"Yes he was but . . . Oh. I see."

"Anyway, I'm not sure that you're going to be in any shape to go riding tomorrow. You're gonna be awful sore."

"I have to get cracking on this case. I've not only got to figure out who killed Monty, but I've also got to find his boy."

"All right," she said, "I'll start heating the bath water and then go down and get you some ice to put on that bad eye."

"Thanks, Rita. I'm sorry that I've caused you so much trouble."

"Don't worry about that. Like I said, just seeing someone whip Ivan for a change was worth any trouble you might cause. And besides, I think I'm going to enjoy getting to know you tonight."

Longarm didn't exactly understand what she meant by that, but he let it slide. He sure wasn't in any condition to make love to a plump and pretty little gal like Rita.

She looked strong and energetic, and he was far too beat up to do her any favors.

"Your bath is ready! Come on into the kitchen and shuck off those smelly clothes. While you're cleaning up, I'll start the chicken and those dumplings that I promised."

Longarm eased out of the chair and brought his glass and what was left of the excellent bottle of whiskey with him. She had a big tin tub of water ready and said, "Here's some soap and a scrub brush."

"I'm supposed to take my bath right here in your kitchen while you cook?"

"Sure. Why not?"

He was blushing. "I don't know, I just . . ."

Rita giggled. "Listen, Marshal Long. You aren't the first man that has taken a bath while I cooked him a good supper. All I ask is that you do your part in carrying on a conversation. It makes the time pass more pleasantly. That, and we share the bottle."

"I'm afraid I've been pretty greedy with it," he said, holding it up to eye level. "I've probably drunk half of it already."

"You can drink it all if you want," Rita said. "I got more where that came from, and I know you're hurting. So don't worry about it. Just undress so I can get those smelly clothes outside."

To emphasize her point, Rita pinched her nostrils with her thumb and forefinger and made a face that caused Longarm to smile.

He unbuckled his gun belt and hooked it over a kitchen chair and then, aware that Rita was watching him a whole lot closer than the plucked chicken she was preparing to dismember, he took off his boots, stockings, shirt and then finally his pants and underwear.

"Whuuh wee!" she exclaimed, snatching up the pale, flaccid chicken by its neck and swing it around, "You are hung like Roanie! My . . . oh . . . my!"

Longarm wasn't unaccustomed to having women see

him naked, but under these unusual circumstances, he felt about as masculine as the poor stewing hen that was being waved about in Rita's excitement. Fast as he could, he plopped down in the tub of water which was hot enough to scald the bristles off a boar hog.

"Ouch!" he cried. "Rita, what are you trying to do . . . boil me to death?"

"Sorry," she said, hurrying over with a pail of water which he tossed into his lap. "That better now?"

"Some," he groaned, sweat breaking out all across his body. His testicles were even turning red.

"Oh," she said, "you just lie back and enjoy yourself while I get this bird to boilin' and then I'll scrub you up and find you a clean nightshirt."

Longarm thought that sounded just fine. "And don't forgot that ice for my eye."

"I'll get it in a minute."

Ten minutes later, Rita was on her knees beside the tub giving his body a vigorous scrubbing with a brush that Longarm thought was altogether too stiff. But he had his whiskey and the woman was doing her best to clean him. Still, when she sent the brush underwater and began to work at his crotch, Longarm had to clamp a strong hand on her wrist and say, "I believe I can do that part and the back part myself, thank you."

"Suit yourself, big boy." Rita gave him a kiss on the lips and plunged her hand into the soapy water to grip his manhood. "I just want to make sure that it's all clean and nice."

"Oh?"

"You about done with soaking?"

He nodded.

"Good. The chicken is stewing in the dumplings, and we have time now."

"For what?"

She winked. "I think you know the answer to that."

Longarm was afraid he did. Rita was a woman that had

no intention of being denied her pound of flesh ... or whatever his manhood weighed. And now, as she began to undress and show him what she had upstairs, he decided that it wouldn't be fair to plead to sexual inability.

"What do you think?" she asked, when she was fully undressed and had pirouetted around in a full circle like a cheerful cherub.

"Not bad at all," he said in all honesty as he stood up in the tub and realized that he was already starting to get a stiff one. "In fact, you're a fine, fine looking woman."

"You bet I am," she agreed, placing her hands on the outsides of her breasts and pushing them together so that they looked even more enormous. "Come on and let's have a little fun before we eat."

She grabbed Longarm's hand, and he almost fell over himself trying to get out of the tub so fast. Next thing he knew, he was being yanked headlong down a little hallway into Rita's bedroom and then was practically thrown across the bed whose covers she had artfully turned back.

"Oh my," she moaned, bending over and taking him in her mouth and then sucking on him like he was a piece of licorice candy. "You are long and sweet!"

Custis didn't know what to say to that so he just closed his eyes and let Rita have her way with him until finally he started to feel an ache down below and knew it was time to get real serious about this lovemaking.

He rolled Rita over and grabbed her legs behind her knees, pushed them up in the air and buried himself in her bush. Rita cried out with pleasure, and Longarm rode her hard until she began to shake and then he dropped her legs and rode her even harder.

"Oh darling!" she cried. "Please don't stop. Don't ever stop!"

"I'll have to sooner or later," he grunted, giving it his very best.

"Then later!"

"All right then," he said between clenched teeth.

Longarm felt the young woman wrap her short but

37

powerful legs around his waist, and when she began to sing like a mockingbird, he let himself go and filled her with his seed while Rita trilled a high, shrill note of ecstasy.

It took them both awhile to get their breath, and then Rita clamped him in a bear hug and smothered his lips with wet kisses. "Boy oh boy," she panted, "are we going to have a good time for a few days."

He didn't want to spoil her party, but felt compelled to warn, "Rita, honey. I'm here on official business. I have to find the killer of my old friend Monty, and I'm really hoping that won't take long."

"But it might take weeks . . . months, even."

"I don't have that long to spare. And I need to find Tyler."

"I know."

"Don't you have any idea who ambushed and killed poor Monty?"

She gazed down into his eyes. "I'll put some more thought to it. Okay?"

"All right."

"But I don't think it was Wade Black."

"What makes you say that?"

"Wade isn't the kind to ambush anyone. If he wanted to kill Monty, he would have given him a fair chance. They'd have gone for their guns, and the best man would have walked away."

"You say that," Longarm answered, "but you forget that killing a lawman is almost certain to earn a man a lifetime in prison or a quick trip to the gallows."

"That's true, but I still don't think Wade is your man. I *know* Wade."

Longarm got the message. The way he figured it, Rita knew Monty, Ivan, a cowboy named Pete, Wade and now himself and probably a whole lot of other men.

"Well," he said after a moment of reflection, "who *don't* you know that might have killed Monty?

"I'm going to put some hard thought to that question,"

she said in an earnest voice. "I loved Monty and whoever killed him has to be brought to justice. But can't we just enjoy ourselves tonight and tomorrow and then the next day? You'll feel a whole lot better, and then you can go off and find Monty's killer."

"All right," Longarm said. "That chicken sure smells good, and I guess I could eat a bunch of them dumplings, too. I feel a little weak, to tell you the truth."

"You'll revive." Rita hopped out of bed and reached for a silk dressing gown. "I'm going to feed you and give you lots of goat's milk."

"Why the goat's milk?"

"I read somewhere in a ladies' magazine that goat's milk makes a man . . . well, it helps him do what a woman wants him to do more often and with more of his love juices."

Longarm couldn't believe what he was hearing. "Go on now!"

"I'm serious. It will make a big difference."

"I do just fine with whiskey."

"Goat's milk." She winked. "I'll make you drink a gallon of it tonight, and you'll think you're stronger than Apollo."

"Cripes, is he even bigger than Ivan?"

"Never mind," Rita said with a laugh. "Just trust me and see if we don't make love at least ten times before sunrise."

"Woman, you're fixing to kill me."

"Yeah," she said, jiggling those beautiful breasts, "but what a way to die!"

Longarm wasn't fit to ride Roanie or to even get dressed the next morning, but he was feeling pretty proud of himself.

Ten times and every one of them long and strong. Not bad, he told himself as he shaved and had a huge breakfast which he washed down with cold goat's milk. He still didn't care for its taste, but he was beginning to think that it did have some powers of sexual rejuvenation.

But after a night of passion, he was ready for Rambunctious Roanie and eager to begin his investigation. So, despite Rita's lamenting and loud protestations, he saddled the roan gelding and went out to talk to Wade Black and some of the other cattlemen.

The Rocking J Ranch was a nice spread, and it was easy to see that Black kept his outfit under a tight rein. The cattle were fat, the water tanks didn't leak, and when Custis trotted into the ranch yard, he could see that the tack room, blacksmith's shop, barn, corrals and the house itself were all in excellent repair.

A handsome woman wearing a calico dress and with her hair tied up in two long pigtails came out to stand on the porch. "Can I help you, Mister?"

"I'm looking for Wade Black."

"He's my brother, and you'll find him out behind the barn working with a colt. But, if you're looking for a job, I'm afraid we're not hiring right now."

"No," Longarm said, tipping his hat. "I'm looking for information."

"Then perhaps I can help you."

"I'd rather speak with your brother. But thanks for your time."

"Don't mention it, Mister . . . ?"

"Long. Custis Long."

"I've never seen you in Mountain City before."

"I'm from Denver."

"I've heard it's a big city. I'd like to visit it someday."

"If you do, maybe we'll meet again," Longarm said with a smile as he reined his horse around and circled the barn.

Wade Black was graceful, with the broadest shoulders Longarm had ever seen on a man. Rakish in appearance, he wore a black handlebar mustache, fancy boots and an expensive blue floral shirt unbuttoned down to the middle of his thick chest. He glanced at Longarm, and then turned back to the skittish colt he was working on a lead line and yelled, "What do you want?"

"I need to talk to you in private," Longarm said, counting three cowboys standing just outside the round corral.

"No time to talk now. Maybe later."

"It's about who murdered Marshal Kilpatrick."

Black scowled, and Longarm heard him utter an expletive, but the man stopped and led the colt over to the corral where one of the cowboys stood. "Bert, work him some more until I finish up talking to this man."

"Yes, sir."

Black ducked through the corral poles and headed back toward the ranch house without even looking to see if Longarm was following along behind. When the rancher came to his front porch, he turned and said, "All right. What is it you want to know about Kilpatrick?"

"He was an old friend of mine, and I want to find out who killed him."

"And you think I might know something?"

Longarm could see that Black operated on a short fuse. Not wanting to antagonize the man, he said, "Monty saved my life once and, after he was shot, he sent me a letter while he lay on his death bed. He asked that I find and bring to justice whoever ambushed him."

"Wish I could help you but I can't," the rancher said as his sister reappeared on the front porch. "Lilly, did you hear what this man just asked me?"

"I did."

"I told him I don't know who killed Monty. You got anything to add to that?"

"Yes," she said, "I think I know who killed him."

Longarm almost fell out of the saddle. "Who?"

"Ivan probably killed him."

Longarm had made a mental note that Ivan might have been involved, although he did not seem like the ambushing type. "Why do you think that?"

"Because he is crazy jealous when any man shows interest in Rita Townsend, and Marshal Kilpatrick was

41

showing real interest just before he was shot."

Longarm nodded in agreement. "Mind if I step down from this horse so we can talk about this?"

"No."

But Wade Black wasn't pleased. "Lilly," he complained, "we discussed this over and over and agreed that we had no proof that Ivan shot the marshal. Given that, I don't think you ought to have said anything to this man who we know absolutely nothing about."

"I'm a federal marshal," Longarm told the pair as he stepped down and then showed them his badge. "I came all the way out here to solve this case and that's what I mean to do."

"In that case," Lilly said, "we'll be glad to tell you anything about the murder that we think might help."

"You tell him," Wade snapped. "I got no time for idle chatter."

Longarm couldn't help but bristle. "I would hardly call a good man's death a matter of idle chatter, Mr. Black."

The rancher's eyes hardened. "Marshal," he said, "you look like someone just beat the hell out of you, and I'd think that, given the shape you are in, you wouldn't be eager to prod a man like myself."

"I'm not prodding you," Longarm said, feeling a growing dislike for the man, "but I *am* seeking information. So why don't you tell me what you know and then you can go about your business?"

Black flushed with anger, but he took a deep breath and forced himself to sound reasonable. "Like I said, I don't know anything but, if I were you, my first suspect would be Ivan Rostovich. The man is a little crazy, and he's mean to the bone. He and I almost got into it one time, and I'd have shot him on the spot if it hadn't been for Marshal Kilpatrick coming between us."

"Then you owe Monty for keeping you out of prison."

Black blinked. "I guess you could say that I do."

"Then can you tell me anyone else that might have had it in for Monty?"

"Maybe Ramon Sanchez who runs a flock of stinking sheep over to the east of us about ten miles. Ramon didn't like the marshal because he thought he was taking sides."

"I heard it said that you thought Marshal Kilpatrick took sides against you and the other cattlemen."

"That's a damned lie!"

"All right," Longarm said. "I'll have a talk with Sanchez as soon as I leave here. Anything else?"

"No. And I've got no more time to waste with your questions," Black said as he turned and stomped off back toward the corral.

"Is he always like that?" Longarm asked. "Or is it just something about my face that he doesn't like?"

Lilly shrugged. "Wade was born angry and losing his wife and daughter in childbirth eight years ago didn't improve his outlook or his disposition."

Longarm tied Roanie to the hitching post and stiffly climbed the stairs to the broad veranda. He was feeling sore from the pounding he'd taken in the fight with Ivan. "Miss Black, I'm sorry about your brother, but it's a waste for a man his age to always be so angry."

"Maybe he likes to be angry," Lilly told him, taking a chair and beckoning Longarm to do the same. "Some men think they have to be tough and angry all the time to get any respect. At least, that's my observation."

Longarm sat down beside her. "I guess you're right. Did you know Marshal Kilpatrick very well?"

"I knew enough to realize he was a very good man. He was out here a few times and I found him to be thoughtful and intelligent. He wasn't angry like Wade, but he was melancholy. He and my brother had both lost their wives and children . . . though the circumstances were quite different. Anyway, they had a bond, and despite what someone must have told you, Monty and my brother were good friends who respected each other very much."

"I'm glad to hear that." Longarm reached up and gingerly touched his still swollen and purplish eye. Not meaning to, he winced.

"What happened to you?" Lilly asked with genuine concern.

"I got into a fight yesterday with Ivan."

Her eyes widened. "Oh my heavens! No wonder you look so bad, but I'm surprised you are even upright. Ivan usually breaks his opponent's bones and lays them up for weeks. That's what he and my brother tangled over."

"What's that?"

"Well, Ivan beat one of our former cowboys half to death when the poor man just happened to think he was in love with Rita Townsend."

"Doesn't surprise me. Do you also think I ought to talk to Mr. Sanchez?"

Lilly shook her head. "There is bad blood between the sheep men and the cattlemen in this country and especially between Ramon and my brother. But neither Ramon nor Wade would murder anyone except in the heat of a bad fight."

"How do you think I might be able to get Ivan to admit that he ambushed Monty?"

"He'd never do that."

Longarm scowled. "The murder took place weeks ago, and the evidence is old. I need something."

"I have a suggestion, but I doubt you'll take it."

"I'm listening."

"All right," Lilly said, "Seduce Miss Townsend, and see if you can draw Ivan into ambushing you."

Longarm couldn't help but smile. "That's one of the worst ideas I ever heard."

"Well, it's the only one I can think of. And anyway, it shouldn't be too hard for you to get Rita into bed. A lot of men have succeeded, including my brother and Marshal Kilpatrick."

Longarm didn't know what to say to that obvious fact, so he stood up and prepared to leave. "I'd better go now."

"Come back and pay me a visit sometime, if you don't get beat up or shot."

"I might do that." Longarm glanced toward the barn.

"But I have a hunch that your brother wouldn't approve."

Lilly's face clouded. "If it's up to him, I'll become an old spinster. I'm always on the lookout for a man big and tough enough to stand up to Wade. Unfortunately, there aren't any around."

"Except for Ivan. Did he ever show an interest in you?"

"Of course! But I slapped his face and made him look like a fool in front of my brother and our cowboys. Now, I'm sure he hates me, which is fine."

"Aren't you afraid that he might try to get even?"

"No," Lilly said. "I'm always here and, when I do go to town, I surround myself with cowboys, so I'm safe."

Her eyes narrowed and she reached out and touched his forearm. "But Marshal Long, if you flaunt your interest in Rita Townsend, I predict that Ivan will try to kill you. After all, he's gotten away with murdering one lawman, and he'll see no reason why he can't get away with murdering a second."

"If he's guilty, he hasn't gotten away with anything," Longarm said. "And although I don't much like your suggestion of making myself his bait, it might be the only way to bring Ivan to justice."

"He's your man," Lilly said. "I can say that without a doubt."

"I hope you're right," Longarm said. "But, over the years, Monty must have made a lot of enemies, any one of which could have finally exacted their revenge."

She wasn't in agreement. "Marshal, have you met Rita yet?"

"I have."

"She's a little on the chubby side but very attractive. You shouldn't have much trouble getting her in bed."

Longarm eased down the stairs this time without grunting or wincing in pain. "Tell me something. Are you always so blunt speaking, and why do you so dislike Miss Townsend?"

Lilly's face hardened. "Because she is a tramp with money, and she looks down upon those who have less."

"And," Longarm said, "because your brother went to bed with her."

"Wade shamed himself and me when he did that!" Lilly lowered her voice. "Rita is a slut who tries to pass herself off as being holier than thou. If there is anything I detest, it's a hypocrite."

"Yes," he said, "I can see that." Longarm untied his reins and managed to mount the roan.

"Isn't that Rita's gelding?" Lilly asked.

"As a matter of fact, it was. But I bought the horse from her yesterday."

"Then you know her better than you let on," Lilly said, a chill edging into her voice.

"I suppose you could say that," Longarm replied a moment before he rode away.

Chapter 5

Although he wasn't feeling that well, it was still early in the day and Longarm decided he might as well ride ten miles and have a talk with Ramon Sanchez. Lilly had been pretty open about her feelings and her opinions concerning Ivan and Sanchez, but Longarm had learned that it always paid to make up your own mind about these matters. Besides, it was too early to return to Mountain City and face Rita, who seemed to be insatiable in bed. For another thing, Roanie needed the exercise. So far, he'd behaved himself, but Longarm could tell that the gelding was still full of piss and vinegar.

It took him just over an hour of hard riding to spot the Sanchez flock. Longarm topped a rise and looked down upon a large expanse of good pasture land surrounded by brushy hills. He saw two men herding the sheep down to a tent camp with the help of dogs. The black and white pair spotted Longarm riding down to meet them and began to bark.

Longarm watched as the shorter of the men hurried to his canvas tent and emerged with a rifle in his hands.

"Friend!" Longarm called out. "Amigo!"

The Mexican either didn't hear over the barking of his dogs or he didn't understand because he levered a shell into the chamber of his carbine and kept the weapon pointed at Longarm.

"Amigo! Friend!"

Longarm kept his hands in plain view as he rode into their camp, and the Mexican with the rifle didn't offer him either a greeting or a smile.

Longarm's Spanish wasn't the best and he expected this to be a difficult interview until the, man, in a thick accent demanded, "What you want, mister?"

"My name is Marshal Custis Long and I'm going to reach for my badge, so don't get trigger happy."

Longarm found his badge and showed it to the sheep man while his dogs circled Roanie. Roanie apparently didn't like dogs and, when one of them nipped at his heels, the gelding kicked and then started bucking. Unfortunately for Longarm, he had been caught off guard and damned if he didn't crash to the earth while the excited dogs badgered the gelding, sending him racing away.

Longarm swore, coming to his feet. "Tell your dogs to leave that horse alone!"

The Mexican whistled shrilly and the dogs broke off their chase as Roanie disappeared over the ridge.

"What you want?" the Mexican again demanded.

"I want to know if you knew Marshal Kilpatrick."

"Sí."

"Did you have any reason to kill him?"

The Mexican's eyes widened, and he stared at Longarm as if he were loco. Finally, he lowered the rifle and yelled at his friend, gesturing toward where Roanie had vanished. The other shepherd took off at a trot and soon disappeared over the ridge.

"Juan will catch your horse," the Mexican said in his thick accent. "Don't worry, senor."

"He'd better catch him," Longarm warned, dusting off his clothes and feeling like he might have reinjured his shoulder. "And keep those dogs under control."

The Mexican shouted at the dogs and then gave them

hand signals. They darted toward the flock of sheep and Longarm watched them each take opposite sides of the flock and then lie down as still as statues.

"Good dogs," the Mexican said, nodding with approval and then taking a sack of tobacco and paper out of his shirt pocket.

Longarm waited until the man had rolled and lit a cigarette, then he said, "Are you Ramon Sanchez?"

"Sí."

"I am trying to find out who murdered my friend, Marshal Monty Kilpatrick. Do you know anything about his death?"

"Your amigo . . . he was my friend too!" Sanchez said earnestly. "He was a good man. I feel very sad when he die. Got very drunk."

"I see. Did any of the other sheep men hate Kilpatrick?"

"No!" the Mexican spat. "Kilpatrick *good* to sheep men. Maybe Senor Black kill him."

"I don't think so," Longarm said. "And anyway, I was just there and talked to him. Is there anyone else that might have killed Marshal Kilpatrick for whatever reason you can think of?"

The Mexican looked away for a long time, and finally, he expelled a stream of smoke from his nostrils and said, "Maybe Mr. Townsend."

The statement set Longarm back on his heels. "Now why would the mayor of Mountain City want to kill his respected and well-liked town marshal?"

Sanchez shrugged his shoulders and smoked faster.

"Look, Mr. Sanchez. You must have had some reason to make that statement."

"No comprendo, senor."

"Sure you *comprende!"* Longarm said, unable to curb his irritation. "Now look, Mr. Sanchez. I've come all the way from Colorado to find out who killed my friend and your marshal. You say he was a good man, and you called him your amigo. If that's true, then I have to know why you say that Mr. Townsend might have killed Monty."

The Mexican needed a distraction and he found it with his dogs. With a series of shrill whistles, he quickly had them bringing his flock in for the night and Longarm had to admit it was a sight to watch the pair work so smoothly together.

"Ramon, I've been told that Ivan probably killed Marshal Kilpatrick. What do you think about that?"

"Sí! Maybe so."

"But also maybe so Mr. Townsend."

Sanchez finally looked him right in the eye. He was probably in his early forties, short and dark with deep lines in his face and hands that were abnormally large given his modest stature. "Maybe Ivan, but maybe Mr. Townsend. That is all I can say."

"But why would Abe Townsend kill Monty who was probably going to ask his daughter to become his wife?"

"Sometimes, senor, a man does not wish to lose his daughter to another man. *Comprende*?"

"Yes," Longarm replied, thinking about what he had seen of the man, and what Rita had told him how her stepfather had always protected her and given her a house and anything she wanted. Could it be possible that Abe Townsend *had* killed Monty?

A half hour later, and without getting any more information or comments from Sanchez, the other sheep man appeared with Roanie.

Longarm checked his cinch and grunted with pain as he stabbed his toe into the stirrup and hauled his carcass back into the saddle.

"Mr. Sanchez, thanks for your time and your words. I'll put some thought to what you said."

"I know nothing. *Nada*," the Mexican said, his face impassive.

"I understand. You don't want me to say anything about your suspicion that it could have been the mayor who shot the marshal."

"Sí . . . or Ivan. He very bad man."

Longarm set himself firmly in the saddle and then he gave Roanie a good boot in the ribs. The gelding was already sweaty from having run away, but Longarm figured the animal could stand some more hard riding so that he wouldn't be so quick to start bucking again.

When he returned to Mountain City, Longarm rode directly to Monty's cabin just west of town. After he had put Roanie in the little corral, Longarm gave the cabin a thorough inspection, hoping he just might come up with something that would give him a clue as to the circumstances leading up to his old friend's ambush and death.

Monty had been a man who appreciated order and the interior of his cabin was neat and tidy. There was a stack of firewood beside the cast-iron stove and Longarm got a fire going as evening shadows fell across the hillsides. Then he found tins of food and prepared himself a simple but adequate supper of corned beef, beans and flapjacks. While his meal was cooking, he went over to Monty's desk and sat down to stare at a neat stack of papers.

Maybe there was something among them that would give him a meaningful clue as to Monty's killer.

Longarm didn't find anything of interest in the stack of papers on Monty's desk, but he sure found plenty to catch his attention in Monty's trash basket, which had been kicked out of sight under the desk. Every piece of wasted paper in the basket had been wadded up in a tight ball, and the very first one Longarm smoothed out and read was a letter from Rita Townsend which read:

> *Dear Monty, I didn't want it to come to this but you HAVE to marry me because I am expecting YOUR child. I should have told you this before but I didn't want it hanging over your head. I wanted you to marry me because you wanted to, not had to. But now you HAVE to so let's stop fighting and set a quick wedding date. Rita*

Longarm reread the letter twice and then he opened and smoothed out the other letters that had been wadded up and discarded. Each of them was really the same letter, just different drafts all saying that Monty didn't believe he was the real father of the child Rita carried. In two of the letters, he actually had written identical lines:

Sorry, Rita, but I don't love you and never will. I still love Henrietta and my son, and I know Ivan is the one who fathered the child you say you carry.

"So," Longarm said out loud. "Rita is with child! But how could that be? She sure didn't seem to act like a pregnant woman last night."

Longarm didn't know about such things, but he did have a hunch that a woman in the early stages of pregnancy not only wouldn't show her condition but could still love making love. So Rita might be with child or the whole thing might just have been a ruse to force Monty into making her an honest woman. Longarm realized that it could be months before he had any real way of knowing if the woman was pregnant or not.

Suddenly, the storm that had been threatening for two days broke, and the wind began to blow and it started to rain hard. Longarm left the smoothed out letters on Monty's desk, and he went to stand in the cabin's open doorway, staring at the lightning and driving rain.

He lit a cheroot and smoked quietly, considering what he had just discovered in his old friend's wastebasket. The crumpled and discarded letters he'd just found didn't prove who killed Monty. But it did raise some interesting questions, and it added a third strong suspect to Longarm's list of potential murderers—Rita Townsend. If Monty had refused to marry her and shamed her by claiming that Ivan, not himself, was the father of the child in her womb, then she would be a scorned woman. *Hell,*

Longarm thought, *even if she wasn't pregnant, she'd feel scorned by Monty's refusal.*

Longarm went back inside and ate his supper, then rummaged around in the cupboards until he found a pint bottle of brandy. He poured himself a couple of shots and went back outside to check on Roanie and then to relight his cheroot and cogitate on this new and important information. In the morning, he'd ride into town and show the letters to Rita and to Ivan and see what developed. Maybe he'd get lucky and one of them would break and reveal themselves to be Monty's killer.

It had rained hard all night, but when Longarm awoke, the sun was shining and the grass out in the meadow glistened with raindrops. Longarm felt a lot better and the swelling of his eye and his hands were greatly reduced. He found hay in the little shed and fed Roanie, then shaved and boiled a pot of strong coffee thinking he'd have breakfast in town.

It was nine o'clock when he rode into Mountain City trying to decide who he should confront first . . . Ivan or Rita. Monty's unfinished letters were folded neatly in his coat pocket, and he tied Roanie to a hitching rail in front of the Copper Skillet Cafe. Feeling optimistic that he could solve this murder case, Longarm went inside and ordered a big breakfast intending to carefully plot his next move.

"Well, hello there, Marshal. Mind if I join you?"

Longarm glanced up from his table to see the mayor. "Not at all. Have a seat. I've ordered breakfast, but it hasn't gotten here yet."

"You picked the best place in town. Are you feeling any better?"

"Much."

Mayor Townsend exchanged greetings with some of the other customers while Longarm sipped his coffee. Finally, Townsend leaned across the table and whispered, "Did you talk to Wade Black yesterday like I suggested?"

53

"As a matter of fact, I did."

Townsend leaned closer. "Well?"

"I don't think he did it."

The mayor rocked back with surprise and dismay. "Why not? I told you he believed Marshal Kilpatrick was playing favorites with the sheep men."

Longarm glanced around the cafe and noticed that everyone in the room had stopped talking. "Mr. Townsend," he said, "don't you think we ought to carry on this conversation in private after we've finished our breakfast?"

The mayor realized what was going on and reluctantly nodded. "I'll be at my store. Come by as soon as you're finished because we sure do need to talk."

"Fine," Longarm said, enjoying his coffee. "But I never like to hurry when I eat, and I've got a big order coming up. Aren't you hungry?"

"I just lost my appetite," Mayor Townsend snapped. "And I'll tell you something else . . . you're getting off on the wrong foot in this here investigation."

"Well," Longarm told the upset man, "maybe you can get me straightened out when we have our talk later this morning."

"I intend to do just that!"

Townsend stomped out of the cafe, and Longarm just shook his head. His breakfast arrived and he dug in with a huge appetite, wondering what Abe Townsend would say if he knew Ramon Sanchez had suggested that the mayor himself might be the real killer.

Chapter 6

"Well hello there, stranger!" Rita said, folding her arms over her ample bosom and tapping her toe on the floor. "Where have you been?"

Longarm glanced over at the mayor, who pretended to be busy with some paperwork at the counter. "I was out doing my business."

"I thought you were coming by last evening for supper."

"It was about to rain, and I decided to just hole up at Monty's cabin. So I fed Roanie and turned in early."

Rita looked as sour-faced as her father, and Longarm couldn't help but wonder how this was all going to unfold this morning. He would have much preferred to have spoken to them separately, but perhaps this would work even better.

"Custis, you look kind of tired," Rita said.

"I feel rested."

"Would you like some coffee? We've got a pot brewing in the store room out back."

"Sure."

It became obvious that Rita wanted him to come with her so they could speak in private, but Longarm decided to hold his ground and to first have a word in private with her father.

"Well?"

"I need to speak to your father for a moment. I'll be right along," he told her.

Rita gave him a disapproving look. Her father said, "Go along, the Marshal and I have a few things to discuss."

"Well," she pouted, "I guess he and I *also* have a few things to discuss. Like why didn't he come back to my house last night and sleep with me after the way we humped most of the night before!"

"Rita! Don't talk like a common slut!" her father ordered.

When the woman stomped off in a huff, Townsend shook his head and confessed, "Sometimes I don't know what to think of Rita. I tried to raise her to be a lady, but it appears that I've failed. I guess a girl needs her mother for an example and Rita's mother was a lady."

"It must have been hard raising Rita by yourself."

"Oh," the mayor said, "it was, but we're really very close. In fact, I don't know what I'd do if Rita ever left Mountain City. She's really all I have to live for now. I've told her that when I retire, she can have this mercantile business, but she just isn't interested. I sure don't understand that. I make a very good living here. There are very few people in town that earn more money than I do."

"Glad to hear that," Longarm said. "So what do you have against Wade Black?"

Townsend's eyes sparked. "Nothing except that he's arrogant and an all around jackass."

"Does he do business with you?"

Townsend's lips tightened down at the corners. "Not anymore."

"What happened between you?"

"That's none of your business."

"I disagree."

Longarm decided it was time to see if he could provoke the man into saying something meaningful. "Was it because Wade refused to marry your daughter?"

There was a pencil in the mayor's hand and it snapped. "Wade thought he was too damned good for her! Oh, but Rita was good enough to take to bed. Just not good enough to marry."

"And what about Marshal Kilpatrick? Did he feel the same?"

Townsend's face turned crimson and he hissed, "That marshal friend of yours wouldn't marry her even after . . . Never mind."

"After what?" Longarm demanded.

"I said never mind!"

"After he impregnated Rita?"

"I . . . I don't want to talk about this anymore." Townsend turned and started to march off, but Longarm stepped into his path. "That's it, isn't it? Marshal Kilpatrick got your daughter pregnant, then refused to marry her and so you killed him."

"What?" The man staggered backward, gripping the counter to keep from falling.

"And," Longarm continued, "you probably did it with Rita's help."

"You're insane!"

"Am I?"

Longarm reached into his inside coat pocket and found the letter that Rita had written demanding that Monty marry her because she was with child. He smoothed it out on the counter and indicated that the mayor was to read it. "What does this tell you?"

Townsend bent over and read the letter. When he was finished, he took a deep breath and said, "This letter means *nothing*."

Townsend tried to turn again and leave, but Longarm grabbed his arm and spun him around hard. He shoved the man up against his counter and said, "That letter tells me that your daughter was desperate for Monty to marry her and give her respectability. It also tells me that the marshal refused."

"That's no evidence that you can use against either me

or my daughter," Townsend argued, his voice ragged with desperation. "Marshal, you are grasping at straws!"

"Am I?" Longarm asked, seeing beads of sweat forming on the mayor's brow. "Well, I have several other letters of correspondence between your daughter and Marshal Kilpatrick. They get even better."

"You're bluffing,"

"Am I?"

"Rita didn't have anything to do with Monty's death!"

"You're going to have to prove that to me."

"It was Ivan that killed the marshal! Ivan is in love with my daughter, and he went insane out of jealousy and killed your friend."

"Can you prove that?" Longarm replied. He decided it was time to run a bluff and added, "Because, if you can't, I'm going to Flagstaff and show these letters to Judge Lawson. I am quite sure that he'll find them highly incriminating. I think he'll order me to arrest your daughter for the murder of Marshal Monty Kilpatrick."

"No!" Townsend wailed. "Listen, if you do that our reputations will be ruined all over Northern Arizona. Please!"

Longarm decided to let the man sweat for a few moments as he pretended to weigh a very difficult decision. Finally, he said, "Mayor, if you help me get a confession out of Ivan, maybe I'll forget Judge Lawson and your daughter's letters."

Townsend reached into his pocket, found his bandana, then used it to mop his sweaty brow. "Ivan is very dangerous. He has a temper that can blow off like a stick of dynamite."

"I know. We had a fight. Remember? So why did Rita ever give in and sleep with someone like that?"

The mayor moaned. "When I discovered what was going on I nearly killed them both."

"Oh?"

"I said *nearly*."

"But you needed Ivan to threaten Monty, hoping to

force him to marry your daughter. Isn't that the truth?"

"Yes," the man whispered, not able to meet Longarm's hard gaze.

"And when the threats didn't work . . . you told Ivan that *he* was the father of the child that Rita was carrying but that she was still going to marry Monty."

"I didn't expect Ivan to kill him! I just wanted Ivan to scare the marshal."

Longarm said, "I could have told you that Monty Kilpatrick wouldn't scare."

"I didn't know that. I swear it," Townsend insisted.

"So let's go get a confession out of Ivan."

"It won't be that easy. He may look stupid, but he isn't."

"Then tell me exactly how we're going to do this," Longarm said, shoving Rita's threatening letter into her father's face.

Townsend swallowed hard and then he reached under his counter and found a bottle. He took several swift and deep gulps, then stammered, "I'll go over to the livery and rile Ivan up just a bit. But I'll only do it on the condition that you'll be hiding somewhere close enough to stop Ivan if he loses his temper and tries to hurt me."

"You can't let that happen before he admits to killing Marshal Kilpatrick."

"I know." Townsend took another drink, then corked the bottle and slid it back under his counter. "I never understood why Kilpatrick refused to marry my daughter. They would have been a fine pair. I even offered to make him an equal partner in this business after he married Rita."

"Monty wouldn't have made a very good businessman," Longarm said. "It just wasn't in him."

"Was it in him to do the right thing and marry the woman he got pregnant?"

"Yes," Longarm answered, "if Monty was absolutely convinced that he was the father of the child she is carrying."

"Of course he was!"

Longarm replaced the letter in his coat pocket and said, "I have another letter here from Monty saying he was sure that it was Ivan who got Rita pregnant."

"That's not true!" the mayor protested. "Why, she told me they only slept together once or twice and that he got her drunk and forced himself upon her."

Longarm doubted that was the case, but held his tongue.

"It *had* to be Kilpatrick," the mayor added, looking desperate.

"Let's go set up Ivan," Longarm told the man, wondering if he could endure the strain of provoking the giant into a confession.

"All right."

"Father!" Rita shouted from the back of the store. "What is . . ."

"The marshal and I have a little job to do," Townsend called. "Honey, we'll be right back."

"Custis!"

"Like your father says, we'll just be a few minutes and then we can talk."

Longarm hustled the mayor outside and propelled the smaller man toward the livery. When they were still some distance from Ivan's place, Longarm said, "Draw Ivan outside in front of his barn, and I'll hide behind that big water trough. Once you get the man to admit his guilt, I'll jump out and arrest him."

"You'd better be quick about it or Ivan might kill me."

"I won't let that happen."

Townsend gulped and nodded. His face was as white as flour, and his eyes round with fear, but he headed for the barn and Longarm trotted over to crouch behind the horse watering trough.

"Ivan!" Townsend called in a voice that quavered. "Ivan! It's Abe. We need to talk."

Ivan appeared a moment later. He was barefooted and

only half dressed, the same as when Longarm had first seen the giant. "Abe, what do you want?"

"It's about my daughter. She's feeling a little poorly, and I figured that you might want to come by later this afternoon and maybe cheer her up some."

Suspicion left the giant's bearded and swollen face. "Yeah, Mr. Townsend." he said, "I'd sure like to do that."

"Good," Townsend said. "You know, Rita talked about you last evening."

"She did?"

"Yes. She said you were a little on the rough side but a good, good man. Rita said . . . well, I think she might be going sweet on you."

Longarm saw Ivan actually smile. "She is? You mean it?"

"I sure do. And I want you to forget the hard things I said to you when I found out you and Rita were sleeping together in your barn."

"Sure," Ivan said, rubbing his huge hands together with boyish anticipation. "I'll take a bath and come by and see Rita in a few minutes."

"You know," Townsend said, trying hard to sound off-handed. "If you hadn't taken care of Marshal Kilpatrick, things just wouldn't have gone good for you and Rita."

Longarm tensed. Here it was, the moment that he needed to put Ivan's thick neck in a noose.

"Yeah," the giant said, looking almost euphoric.

Townsend mopped his brow and set his snare once more. "I mean, if Marshal Kilpatrick was still alive, Rita would be talking about him, instead of you and that would have been a damned pity."

"I'd have killed Marshal Kilpatrick," Ivan vowed, "even if you hadn't paid me to do it."

Longarm heard those words as clearly as if they'd been shouted in his ear. He saw the mayor's face turn even paler and then the man stammered, "I didn't pay you to kill Marshal Kilpatrick!"

Ivan shrugged his massive shoulders with indifference.

"Rita said you did when she gave me the money."

"No!" Townsend cried. "You're lying! Rita never gave you any money!"

"Yes she did, and she ain't got that kind of money on her own. She said . . ."

Townsend lost his fear and became enraged. "Shut up, you lying idiot! You killed Marshal Kilpatrick all on your own."

"She paid me to do it and said you gave her the money."

"Liar!" the mayor screamed, lunging at Ivan.

Ivan reached out and grabbed the much smaller man by the throat. Longarm heard an ominous crack of bone. "Stop!" he shouted, jumping up with his gun in his fist.

Ivan clamped Townsend's limp body to his chest and, using his limp body as a shield, backed into his livery. Although Longarm figured the mayor's neck was broken, he couldn't risk taking Townsend's life.

"Give up!" Longarm ordered racing to the barn door and peering into the darkness. "Ivan!"

"I'll never be hanged!" the giant bellowed from inside. "You go away, or I'll kill Mr. Townsend."

"Abe?" Longarm yelled. "Can you hear me?"

There was no answer so Longarm shouted again. "Abe!"

"I knocked him out," Ivan said. "You better come inside and get him before I do him even more harm."

Longarm hadn't stayed alive this long by being a complete fool. And unless he missed his bet, Ivan was waiting to kill him with a pitchfork or even a gun.

"Ivan, give it up and come out with your hands over your head!"

At that moment, Rita came rushing up to Longarm and cried, "What's going on? Where's my father?"

"Ivan has him inside. I think he's already dead."

Rita cried out and, before Longarm could stop her, she rushed into the barn. There were two quick shots, and then a strangled cry unlike anything that Longarm had ever heard in his life. It wasn't Rita who began to wail, it was Ivan.

Longarm crouched low, fearing the worst. He entered the barn in a rush, and when he saw Ivan's unmistakably huge silhouette, Longarm opened fire, because he knew that the liveryman was armed and insane with grief.

The giant took three bullets and rolled over backward with his bare heels drumming the hard-packed earth. Then, he became still.

Longarm had a sick feeling building up inside. Moments later, as he knelt in the musty gloom and checked pulses, he confirmed his worst fears ... Mayor Abe Townsend, Rita Townsend and Ivan Rostovich were *all* dead.

Chapter 7

Mountain City was in an uproar over the three killings, and its town council held an emergency meeting, then rushed out to Monty's cabin to have a few strong words with Longarm.

"Marshal Long," a short, heavyset man in his sixties with a walrus mustache and a frayed flannel suit declared, "I'm a city councilman and now acting Mayor Stuart Hooter." He jerked a thumb over his shoulder at the collection of men crowded up close behind him. "And these gentlemen are all on our city council."

"Mr. Hooter," Longarm said, "it's a bit cramped inside this cabin. Why don't we do our talking outdoors?"

"What we have to say will be short but not very sweet," Hooter warned.

"All right," Longarm said, escorting them out to the little pole corral, then hooking his heel over the lower rail and leaning up against the fence, "let's hear what you fellas have on your mind."

"What we have on our minds," Hooter snapped, "is that we recently lost our town marshal, our mayor and our blacksmith."

"My regrets," Longarm said evenly, "on losing Marshal Kilpatrick and Miss Townsend. As for your mayor and your blacksmith, they got what they had coming."

"So you say!"

"Look," Custis said, feeling a rising impatience, "Mayor Townsend paid Ivan to ambush and kill Marshal Kilpatrick. And Miss Townsend was far less than an innocent bystander in the whole sorry affair. Now, do you gentlemen have any important business that we should discuss . . . or is this just a show you're putting on for the voters?"

Hooter had large, bushy eyebrows and they shot up with indignation. "I think," he said in a voice that shook with emotion, "you owe us and Mountain City a solution to our problem."

"Which is?"

"Which is we have no more law in our good town and, because of you, Mountain City now has a very bloody reputation!"

"I can't help you," Longarm told the men. "I came out here from Denver to find out who killed Monty Kilpatrick and to bring them to justice. I've done that and I'll soon be leaving."

"Just like that?" one of the councilman cried. "Without first finding a replacement for Marshal Kilpatrick?"

"That's right."

"Sir!" Hooter vigorously protested. "I demand to know the name of your superior in Denver."

"His name is Marshal Billy Vail, and he is in the U.S. Marshal's Office next door to the Denver Mint. Now, if you will excuse me, I'm preparing to take my leave."

"Where are you going?" Hooter demanded.

"I'm going to honor my late friend's dying wish and find his son, Tyler Kilpatrick."

The new town mayor and his friends on the city council had a lot more to say, but Longarm turned on his heel and went back into Monty's cabin and closed the door. A few minutes later, he heard them depart and he finished his packing. Monty had some personal things that Longarm figured Tyler might appreciate as keepsakes, even though the boy had never really known his father.

After making his preparations, Longarm cooked his midday meal and laid down to take a short nap before he hit the trail west toward the Colorado River in search of the boy. He must have been a lot more tired than he'd realized, because it was nearly dark when he was awakened by a knock on Monty's heavy plank door.

Longarm rolled into a sitting position and reached for his gun. "Who is it?"

"It's Lilly Black from the Rocking J Ranch."

Longarm relaxed. "Come on in."

"Are you presentable?"

"No more or less than usual," Custis replied, running his fingers through his long black hair and coming to his feet.

Lilly opened the door and leaned against the jamb. "I thought you might be gone, but then I saw the roan gelding and knew you were still here. I have something important to tell you."

"I'm listening."

"You said that you were going to search for Tyler Kilpatrick."

"That's right." Longarm holstered his gun and pushed to his feet, stifling a yawn. "So what is it that you can tell me?"

"I know the name of Henrietta's sister. The one that most likely took charge of Tyler after his mother's death. That would be a big help, wouldn't it?"

Longarm woke up fast. "Sure it would. What's her name?"

"Not so fast," said Lilly, coming inside. "Before I help you, I want you to help me."

"To do what?"

"I want to leave Mountain City."

"Then leave."

"It's not that simple. Wade is not about to let that happen."

Longarm didn't understand. "Why not?"

"Because he thinks that I'm a little crazy and, if I ever left the Rocking J, he would believe it was because I had a nervous breakdown and was irrational and in need of his help."

"Can't you just tell him you'd like to leave for a while?"

"I've tried, but he won't listen. And since he lost his wife, my brother has come to rely on me far too much. He would never let me go of my own free will."

"Look," Longarm said, trying to sort this conversation out, "what has this to do with you telling me the name of Henrietta's sister?"

"I not only know her name, but I know where she was last living with Tyler."

"And?" Longarm demanded.

Lilly folded her arms across her bosom and raised her chin. "And in exchange for that information, I want you to take me away with you."

Longarm could see that the woman was dead serious. "What I'd rather do," he finally said, "is to just go have a word with your brother. We can go back to the Rocking J together and simply explain . . ."

"He won't listen," Lilly interrupted. "I know Wade. He's lost his wife and child, and I'm the only family he has left. And do you know what that means?"

"I think I can guess."

Lilly closed the door behind her and walked right into Custis's arms. She laid her head on his chest and whispered, "It means that I'm a *prisoner* on that ranch. That I can't be called upon by suitors and that my only fate is to become a dried up old spinster!"

"No one can make someone else their prisoner," Longarm told the handsome but distraught woman. "So I guess I wouldn't be breaking any law if you wanted to come along with me to find Tyler."

"I'll swear that I'll be a big help." Lilly eased out of his grasp and her eyes shone with happiness. "You won't be sorry that you agreed to take me along with you."

"What about Wade?" he asked. "I've got enough to worry about without having to keep looking over my shoulder expecting to see your brother and his cowboys coming after me with blood in their eyes."

"He won't follow us."

Longarm was less than convinced of those words. "If Wade needs you as bad as you say he does, I expect that he might well take up our trail."

"I'll leave him a note tonight and explain that I'm just going away for a while. That I'll be back when I've had a chance to clear my head. Wade will accept that. He knows that I do love the Rocking J Ranch. He just doesn't know how lonely I am."

"Okay," Longarm said. "But, if you're lying about knowing where we can find Tyler, I'm not going to take it like a gentleman."

"I'm not lying. He's over on the Colorado River. Not only do I know the name of the town, but I know his aunt's full name."

She looked up into his eyes. "Marshal Long, without my help, you don't even know where to begin your search. But, with my help, you'll find the little Kilpatrick boy in no time at all."

"Then we'll leave first thing tomorrow," he said, knowing that she was right.

"Custis, I need to ride back to the ranch, gather a few things and sneak out after Wade and the cowboys have fallen asleep. I'll be back shortly after midnight, and by the time Wade realizes I'm missing, we'll be boarding the westbound train out of Flagstaff."

"That sounds good. Bring your own traveling funds."

For the first time since her arrival, Lilly smiled. "What's the matter? Can't the government even afford to buy a poor woman a lousy train ticket?"

"You're not a 'poor woman' and I'm sure that you can well afford to buy your own ticket."

"You're right," Lilly told him. "I've been squirreling

69

my escape money for the last couple of years, and I could buy us a private railroad coach."

"Then it's settled," he said. "Go on back to the Rocking J before your brother gets suspicious, and I'll see you in a few hours."

Lilly's eyes shone bright with anticipation and she kissed him full on the lips before she whirled and ran back outside to her horse. Moments later, Longarm heard the receding drum of hoof beats.

"I'll be damned," he said to himself as he lit his stove and prepared to cook a good traveling meal. "Maybe the search for little Tyler isn't going to be so tough after all."

True to her word, Lilly showed up just after midnight with her saddlebags packed and a small traveling kit tied to her saddle. Longarm had eaten well, taken another nap and Roanie was saddled and ready to ride. As they galloped down the road toward Flagstaff, the air was cool and the night sky glittered with stars that hugged a thin wedge of a silvery moon.

Roanie was feeling frisky and wanted to get his head down between his legs and buck, but Longarm kept him on a tight rein and, after several miles, the gelding grew tired enough to behave.

"I'm going to miss this roan," Longarm said when they stopped to let their horses drink in a noisy little stream that meandered through a grassy meadow filled with wild flowers. "Rita said he was a handful, but I think he just needed some exercise. You're also riding a fine animal."

"Her name is Misty," Lilly told him. "I bought her as a yearling and broke her myself. I wouldn't think of riding another horse."

"Then I guess we'll both be sad to have to leave them in Flagstaff when we board the westbound train."

"We won't have to do that," Lilly told him. "The train pulls out just after six o'clock, and we'll have time to load both our horses in a stock car. They'll travel as far as we're going."

"I thought it was really expensive to put livestock on the train."

"It is, but a good horse is worth keeping. Besides, where we're going, we'd just have to buy another pair and that doesn't make any sense."

"If you've got the money, then it's fine with me."

"Custis, we've got a little extra time to kill. I really don't want to arrive in Flagstaff early," Lilly explained. "The fewer people that see us load our horses and board that westbound . . . the better."

That made sense to Longarm. "Then let's hobble the horses and let them graze. If they're riding the rails all the way to the Colorado River, they're going to need their bellies full of fresh mountain water and grass."

"That's a fine idea."

A few minutes later, with the horses hobbled and chomping the sweet meadow grass as if it were candy, Longarm and Lilly stretched out beside the stream and gazed up at the stars.

"You know," Custis said, "I always felt that you were a whole lot closer to heaven when you were up here in the high mountains. The stars look almost twice as big as they do down in the low country."

"I know," she said. "Mountain skies are beautiful day or night. And you see more shooting stars up here than you do in the desert. At least, that's what I've been told."

He leaned over on one elbow. "Have you ever been anywhere other than in these mountains?"

"No. Wade has, and our father had traveled all over the West. I've read about other places and longed to travel, but that hasn't been possible . . . until now. I'll probably return in a few weeks or a month out of being homesick, but I desperately needed a change in scenery."

"The desert where we're going is a hard place," Longarm said. "You might want to climb back on the train and hurry home."

"I don't know about that. Alone, I might. But with you at my side, I think I'll love even the desert."

Longarm felt her leaning closer. He could smell and almost taste this lonely woman, and he sympathized with her plight. She was far too pretty and young to be a captive on her own cattle ranch.

"Custis," she breathed, "I don't know how to thank you enough for taking me out of here."

"Oh," he said, thinking of several ways she could repay him, none of which had to do with money, "don't worry about it. I'm helping you and you're helping me find Tyler."

"That boy means a lot to you, huh?"

"It's not that he means so much to me," Longarm tried to explain, "but he was Monty's boy, and I just have to make sure that he's happy and being well taken care of. If his aunt is bringing him up right, then I'll feel that I've done my right by Monty."

"And doing 'right' is very important to you, isn't it?"

"Yes," he said. "If a man can't keep his word to a dying friend, then he isn't much of a man."

"I'll bet you're *all* man," she breathed, a moment before their lips met.

Making love in a meadow hadn't been in Longarm's plans but, once she pushed herself tight up against him and her tongue entered his mouth, Longarm decided that it always paid for a man to keep his plans flexible. And although the air was decidedly on the chilly side, neither of them took notice as they tore off their clothes and he mounted her in the field of sweet grass and flowers.

"Oh my heavens!" Lilly gasped when his throbbing manhood pushed deep inside her warm and eager honey pot. "I just saw a shooting star and made a wish, but it sure wasn't any better than this!"

"Good!" he grunted, loving the hot, wet feel of being deep inside Lilly. She wasn't a virgin, but she almost felt as tight as one, and Longarm was glad that he'd removed his pants or he'd have ruined them with grass stains.

Lilly lost herself in their lovemaking. She bucked like a filly and howled like a she-wolf at the silvery slice of

72

moon until Longarm brought her to a shuddering state of ecstasy. Moments later, he took her with a hot, rushing roaring in his throat that carried far through the silent pines.

Later, as they checked their cinches and slapped grass and flowers from their clothing, Lilly threw her head back and laughed long and loud.

"What's so funny?" he asked.

"I was just thinking of what Wade would say if he had seen us rooting up this meadow."

Longarm finished checking his saddle's cinch, and then the Colt that he wore on his hip and finally the hideout derringer attached to his Ingersol railroad watch. He was thinking of a vengeful Wade Black and he didn't feel like joining Lilly's wild, crazy laughter.

Chapter 8

Longarm and Lilly loaded their horses into a stock car just as the sun peeked over the eastern horizon. One of the railroad employees slammed and bolted the gate and said, "We'll stop for water, and I'll make sure they're taken care of when we get down to Truxton. You don't have to worry a thing about those horses. They'll be just fine."

"That's good to know," Lilly said as the steam engine gave a long, mournful wail telling everyone that it was time to board.

"Right on time this morning," the man said. "I hope you have a pleasant ride down into the low country."

"We will," Longarm said, taking Lilly's arm and escorting her toward an anxious conductor who was waving for the last of the morning's passengers to get on board.

"Here are our tickets," Lilly said, handing them to the conductor.

He punched the tickets and said, "Two first-class coach to Needles, California."

"So that's where Tyler is, huh?" Longarm said as he gave Lilly a hand up into the coach. "Needles."

"No," Lilly said, as they started down the aisle in the first-class coach. "But it's the closest the railroad comes to where we can find that boy."

"I don't see why you have to be so secretive," Longarm complained.

"I just don't want you to get the idea that you can find Tyler Kilpatrick without me."

"It never entered my mind."

"Of course it did," Lilly said. "You told me that you always work alone."

They took their seats and were practically the only passengers in the plush coach with its red velvet drapes and upholstered seats trimmed with polished wood and brass.

"I do work alone," Longarm explained. "But this is different because I'm not expecting any trouble . . . unless your brother shows up and decides to go crazy."

"He won't," Lilly assured him. "Wade doesn't trust anyone to run the ranch, so he'll stick right there. Stop worrying."

A young and eager porter dressed in a starched white uniform appeared. "Breakfast will be served in the dining car starting in one hour. If there is anything I can do to make you folks more comfortable, please let me know."

Longarm knew he was going to be hungry. "We'll be there."

"Very good, sir."

The porter vanished, and Longarm gazed out at Flagstaff just as their train lurched forward, steam whistle blowing and smoke billowing from her stack. Longarm watched as the town slowly receded into the smoke. He turned to Lilly and said, "If I recall, Needles is on the Colorado River. It's hot and it's dry."

"So I've heard."

Longarm could see that Lilly wasn't going to give him any information, so he removed his hat and settled back into his soft seat with a contented sigh. Closing his eyes and thinking that he might take a short nap while waiting for the dining car to open, he said, "This first class is really the way to travel."

"If you stick with me," Lilly promised, hand coming to

76

rest on his leg close to his manhood, "we could both get used to the good life."

He chuckled. "Until your money ran out?"

"That would be awhile if I sold my half of the Rocking J."

"Who would buy it other than your brother?"

"No one," she replied. "But Wade would give me a fair buy out. He's a hard man, but he's never been a skinflint, and he wouldn't cheat his sister. Custis, you could do a lot worse than to marry me."

His eyes popped open. "Who said anything about getting married?"

"No one," she answered, "but it doesn't hurt to be thinking of these things . . . just in case."

"In case what?"

"We decide that we would be good for each other."

Longarm looked sideways at the woman. She was attractive, strong and appealing on many levels, but he sure didn't want to get married. "Lilly, put that idea away. I'm not the marrying kind."

"You don't know that for sure until you've tried it. And besides, you're much too talented and capable to remain just a federal marshal all your life."

"I like being a lawman."

"You'd like being my husband better. After we find Tyler and make sure that he's being taken care of, we could settle up with Wade and spend a year or two traveling. That's what I'd most like to do. I'd like to see San Francisco, the Pacific Ocean, Seattle and then travel abroad. Have you ever been abroad?"

"You mean to Europe?"

"Or Asia or the Sandwich Islands." Lilly's eyes shone with excitement. "Think of all the different cultures that are waiting to fascinate and delight us. And imagine all the strange animals we haven't seen, as well as the natural and man-made wonders waiting to be discovered!"

Longarm shook his head. "I have trouble enough figuring out my own world without going to places where the people look and act completely different. I've met Chinese, Basque and Frenchmen. Not only do they speak a different language, they even *think* different."

Lilly shook her head with obvious disappointment. "Custis, I thought you were more adventuresome. I thought you'd be as curious as myself to see far away places."

"There's still a few spots in the West that I've never seen, and I haven't been to see much of Canada, Mexico or Alaska."

"Then we could start with those places and work our way out," Lilly said, as if the matter were settled.

Longarm had to admit the idea was tempting. And he did have a yearning to travel to new locations. "We can start by finding Tyler, but then I've got another matter to look into before I return to Denver."

"What is it?"

"Have you ever heard of a town called Paradise, Arizona?"

"Yes, as a matter of fact."

"Where is it?"

Lilly's brow furrowed. "I think it's along the Colorado. Maybe all the way down toward the Yuma Crossing. Why do you ask?"

"There's this federal Marshal named Boone who is said to be extorting money from the local merchants and doing other things that cast a bad light on our agency. In order to write off my travel expenses, I agreed to find Boone in Paradise and see if the charges are true or not."

"And if they are?"

"Then I'll wire my boss in Denver and explain the circumstances. He'll probably talk to the director of our agency and decisions will be made. I expect what would happen is that I'd get a telegram ordering me to gather information against Marshal Boone and then to arrest the man. He'd be fired and the locals would determine what punishment he would receive based on his crimes."

"I would think," Lilly said, "arresting one of your own

marshals would be a very unpleasant task."

"It would be," Longarm admitted, "and I sure hope it doesn't come to that, but I'd have to do what I was ordered."

"Even if it meant killing Boone?"

"I expect it won't come to that."

"But, if it did?"

"I've sworn to uphold the law," Custis said quietly. "And there are times when that means I have to use a gun to get the job done."

She studied him for several minutes. "I know what happened in Mountain City wasn't your fault. Ivan was bad to the bone and . . . well, I don't know about the Townsends, but I never did trust them."

"What happened back there wasn't how I wanted it to go," Longarm said. "But sometimes things are beyond our control. When that happens you just have to do your best."

"Do you worry about getting killed?"

"I worry about being injured so bad that I could never fully recover. There was a marshal I knew that was shot in the back and paralyzed from the waist down. He killed himself after a few years because his wife left him for another man. People used to feel sorry for Calvin and that, as much as his wife leaving, broke his spirit."

"If you fear being crippled or paralyzed, why stay in this line of work?" Lilly asked. "You know the risks."

"Yeah, I know 'em. But I'm good at what I do, and I like the fact that I never go out on an assignment without feeling excited, but also a little afraid. Nothing works exactly like you expect in my line of work, so it forces you to stay sharp mentally and physically. You can't let down and become lax or you'll fail and maybe die."

"So what is it that keeps you going? The thrill of the hunt?"

"I guess so." Longarm hadn't thought of it that way, but he supposed it was true. There was no more dangerous quarry than a man, especially one that was cunning and experienced.

"I can't possibly understand that, but I'll try to put this very plainly. I'm terribly attracted to you, Custis. I might even be falling in love with you. And I want you to share the adventure of travel with me. When we finish up our business here in Arizona, let's go to California and then on to new and exciting places."

"I don't think I can do it," he told her.

"At least give it some thought. Why not take a year's leave of absence or just tell your superiors that you are stepping back to consider other alternatives."

"They wouldn't be pleased to hear that."

"Who cares?" Lilly asked. "We only live once, so why pass up the chance to explore?"

"Let's see how it goes," Custis told her. "Hell, we might not even be able to stand each other by the time we find Tyler."

Her hand came to rest over his manhood. "I doubt that very much. Don't you?"

"I guess I do," he agreed feeling a little foolish but also aroused. "Doesn't first class mean we get a private compartment?"

"It sure does."

"Then let's go find it," Longarm said, suddenly wanting Lilly in the worst way.

Needles was hot, and it didn't have much appeal to Longarm. As soon as their train stopped, they unloaded then watered their horses. The town itself was a collection of rock, brush and other poorly constructed houses with a few businesses that catered to people making the desert overland crossing and those coming up and down the river on boats and barges.

"North or south?" Longarm asked.

"South," she told him as she mounted her horse. "But I'm not sure how far."

"What's the name of the town where you think Tyler is staying with his aunt?"

"Are you sure you won't try to leave me in this hellhole once you find out where the boy was last known to be living?"

"I'm sure."

"He lives on the river in a little settlement called Topoki."

"Sounds like an Indian name for something," Longarm muttered, feeling a trickle of sweat run down his backbone. He didn't know what the temperature was, but he felt certain it was well over one hundred degrees.

"It might be an Indian name," Lilly agreed. "What I do know is that it is a river crossing and not worthy of calling a town."

"How do you know this if you've never been here?"

"I knew Henrietta, and she told me long ago that she and her sister had inherited a little land at Topoki. She said it had some value because it was a major crossing on the Colorado. I guess there is quicksand and the currents can be pretty treacherous down here, but it's always safe to cross at Topoki."

Longarm gazed out at the sage and barren rock. He found it hard to imagine that anyone could survive in this hard desert land. But he knew that the Mohave, the Yumas and several other tribes somehow eked out a living and that some whites had began to farm along the river by diverting water into their fields.

Just as the trainman who had helped them unload their horses started to climb back on board, Longarm shouted, "Hey mister, do you know how far it is downriver to Topoki?"

"About twenty miles. You can't miss it, because there isn't anything between there and here except rattlesnakes, mosquitoes, scorpions and buzzards."

"Twenty miles," Longarm said, glancing up at the late afternoon sun. "That means we probably won't get there before dark."

"I'd say you're right," the trainman replied, using his bandana to wipe his sweaty brow. "Can't imagine why you two are going that way. You won't find a decent hotel, saloon or restaurant until you get all the way down to the Yuma Crossing."

"Thanks," Lilly said.

"Don't mention it. And, if you take my advice, you'll tie your horses up real short and hobble them as well because the river Indians down here will try to steal them for sure. Down in this country, they don't use 'em to ride . . . they eat 'em just like their brothers, the Apache."

"We'll take your advice," Longarm told the man. "Is there anywhere here that I can buy a Winchester repeating rifle?"

"They ought to sell you one at Clem's Merchantile just up the street. Better make sure that it shoots straight before you give Clem your money, though. He's as crooked as a sidewinder."

Just then, the train gave a loud blast on its whistle and jolted forward. Longarm and Lilly waved good-bye to the helpful man and then rode slowly up the baking street until they came to Clem's.

"I'll stay out here with our horses and gear," Lilly said. "Just get the rifle and whatever you need quick before I roast."

"Don't worry," Longarm told her. "I won't sit and chat in there."

He dismounted and handed his reins to Lilly before he marched into the store which had wooden sides but a ragged canvas ceiling.

"Can I help you?" asked a dirty man in bib overalls without a shirt.

"Are you Clem?"

"Sure am! And who might you be?"

"I'm a fella that needs to buy a good rifle, and I'd prefer a Winchester repeater. What have you got?"

"I've got three of 'em and one is a dandy. Nearly brand new, and I can let you have it for a good price."

"Let's see 'em all," Longarm told the man.

Clem brought out the three rifles and, after a few minutes of hard bargaining, Longarm took the newer weapon and followed Clem out the back door of his business. The merchant looked annoyed. "I don't see why you gotta shoot the darned thing, mister. Anyone can see it's hardly been fired."

"All the more reason to test it out," Longarm replied. "Is it loaded?"

"Sure. Wouldn't be much good empty, now would it?"

Longarm saw a tin can resting about twenty-five yards down the alley. He took careful aim and fired, but missed by a good yard.

"You probably ain't shot much in this kind of heat," Clem said by way of explanation. "It tends to make shooting a little bit tricky."

Longarm sighted and aimed but again missed to the right by the same yard. He handed the rifle back to Clem saying, "It looks good, but it won't do."

"You just have to sight it in and allow for the heat," Clem argued.

"I'll try the other pair you have inside. If they don't shoot any straighter than that rifle, then I'll be on my way."

"If you don't have a rifle out in this country, you could be be sorry and dead."

Longarm couldn't argue the fact. Out here in the desert, the open distances were considerable and, if a man were jumped by outlaws or Indians, he'd better be well armed.

He test fired both of the other rifles and one of them was a little rough looking, but it worked to his satisfaction and shot true to his aim.

"How much for this old rifle?"

"Forty-five."

"Forty dollars, and that's my final offer."

"You're a hard man to deal with," Clem said, "but cash is at a premium in this country, so I'll let you skin me today."

Longarm paid for the weapon and let himself get skinned on a box of ammunition, which improved Clem's sour mood. As he was leaving, Longarm asked, "Do you know where I can find Paradise?"

The store keeper laughed, and it wasn't pretty. "Well, if you're talking about Arizona's Paradise, then sure. It's downriver about a hundred and fifty miles. Hard, dangerous country."

"That's what I was afraid you were going to say," Longarm told the man as he started to leave.

"Say," Clem called, "is that woman out in front going all the way down to Paradise with you?"

"I don't think so. She's probably only going as far as Topoki."

"There ain't even as much there as there is in Paradise."

"We'll see," Longarm told the man as he headed out into the brutal desert heat to rejoin Lilly, who was already flushed and looking distressed.

"You're going to get yourselves in a pack of trouble if you ride out with that woman!" Clem called from his doorway. "This country don't like pretty woman. It'll kill 'em!"

Longarm saw the alarm in Lilly's face, but also heard the fierce determination in her voice when she shouted, "It won't kill me!"

The storekeeper just shook his head and disappeared.

"So you got a rifle," Lilly said. "You should have bought one for me."

"I figured you could buy your own."

Lilly gave him a hard look and then dismounted. "I believe I'll do just that!"

"Don't buy the best looking one," Longarm said, taking the reins to her mare. "Buy the older Winchester. It shoots straighter."

Lilly marched into Clem's store, and Longarm heard rifle shots a few minutes later. Soon, she reappeared with the rifle he'd told her to buy and a box of her own bullets.

"How much did you pay?" he asked, taking the weapon and giving her back her reins.

"Thirty-five dollars. How much did *you* pay?"

"It don't matter," he snapped as he shoved the rifle back into her hands and rode away.

"You paid Clem more than I did. Admit it!"

Longarm touched his heels to Roanie's flanks and sent the gelding trotting south along a riverside trail. If there was anything he hated, it was to be bested by a woman.

Chapter 9

It was slow going along the twisting bank of the Colorado. Not a mile went by that they didn't have to skirt some slough filled with cattails and water plants. And when Longarm and Lilly became impatient and tried to ford the stagnant inlets, they often found their horses floundering in heavy mud up to their bellies or even trying to escape patches of deadly quicksand.

The mosquitoes were ferocious, and they saw plenty of rattlesnakes curled in under the mesquite and water-loving cottonwood and paloverde trees. Egrets and white cranes competed with foxes, wildcats and other animals for food, and the air had the taste of death and decay.

"I can't imagine living down here even with all this water," Lilly said when they stopped on a sandy beach to give the horses a rest and drink. "This river seems as if it has no purpose except to torment."

"The Colorado forms high up in the Rocky Mountains just west of the Continental Divide," Longarm told her. "A place called Spirit Lake, which is the spiritual home of the Ute Indians. And it comes down the western slope and joins the Green River in Grand Junction, then flows down through the desert until it plunges into the Grand Canyon. By the time it gets here, it's been on a long, long journey. All the energy and life seems to have been sucked out of it by the desert heat."

"I can understand that," she said. "I feel as if my life is being sucked dry by this horrible heat. I've never sweated so much in my life."

Longarm uncorked his canteen. "We have to try and remember to drink a lot of water or we'll get cramps . . . or worse."

He drank deeply and then passed the canteen to Lilly who asked, "Doesn't this river end up in the Gulf of California?"

"That's right. It flows through Yuma and then into Mexico. In the spring, it floods all along here, which is why you can see the remnants of scum and driftwood up higher on the hillsides and upper banks."

Longarm studied the sun as it touched the hard, barren mountains to the west, far across the wide river and deep into California's Mohave Desert. "We need to start thinking about finding a good place to camp. One near the river where there's some grass to feed our horses and where we can swim."

"Swim?" Lilly looked appalled. "In that muddy river?"

"Believe me," Longarm told her. "Getting into the water, muddy or not, will be a welcome relief from this heat. It's going to cool down tonight, but the temperature still won't drop much below ninety."

Lilly groaned and raised her hands toward the sky in a gesture of supplication. "Take me back to my high mountain Rocking J Ranch!"

"You wanted to come, and you must have known that it would be this hot," Longarm told her.

"I knew it would be hot, but not hellishly hot."

Longarm retrieved his canteen and continued along the river's bank. They skirted two more sloughs of warm, stagnant water and then came to a beach littered with tiny shells. There was a thin, green sliver of grass along the shore and the mosquitoes and gnats seemed less pesky here than at other sites he'd seen, so he said, "Let's hobble and unsaddle the horses. This is as good as any place to make camp."

"It's horrible," she said, eyes searching under the trees and brush for the dreaded rattlesnakes which grew so large in this low country. "Will the snakes came out and get us tonight?"

"Not likely," Longarm said. "I expect the worst things we have to fear are scorpions and skunks."

"What about Indians?"

"I haven't seen any signs of them, but I'm sure there are some around these parts."

"Maybe we should take turns as sentries."

"That wouldn't be a bad idea," Longarm told her as he unsaddled his horse and prepared to settle in for the night. He unrolled his blanket on the sandy, shelled beach and then quickly undressed. His clothes were soaked with sweat, and he knew that he smelled worse than any mule skinner. "I'm getting cooled down in that water right now."

Kicking off his boots, socks and the last stitch of clothing, Longarm waded rapidly out into the river. The water was warm on the surface but as he waded deeper into the lazy current, he could feel its underlying coolness. His tender feet struggled for purchase in the mud and on the slippery hidden river rocks. When the current reached to his waist, he dove into the river and swam underwater for about a minute before surfacing some thirty or forty yards downriver. Apparently, he had underestimated the river's power. But he was a strong swimmer and soon was back on sound footing.

Looking up river, he cupped his hands to his lips and shouted, "Hey, Lilly, come on in! The water feels fine!"

Lilly started undressing, and when she was buck naked, she very tentatively waded out into the river coming towards Longarm. She yelled something that he didn't hear because his attention was suddenly focused on a movement in the brush near where their horses were grazing.

"Lilly!" he yelled, starting to buck the current as he struggled toward shore. "Get the guns!"

She whirled around just in time to see four lithe brown bodies burst from the mesquite and race for the horses. Both animals bolted in fear and tried to run away, but the Indians were quick and managed to grab their halters.

Lilly was no fool. She knew that, without horses, they were in a bad situation. Not worried about modesty, but only about survival, she ran out of the Colorado and managed to reach Longarm's six-gun and their Winchesters just as one of the Indians broke from the horse-catching effort and met her on the bank.

Longarm struggled with all of his being to reach them as the pair went down on the grass, each fighting to control the other and get possession of the weapons. Longarm watched as the Indian shouted for help and then Lilly tore the Colt from Longarm's holster and pointed it at the thieves. She shouted a warning and the little fella that she had wrestled with dived into the brush and vanished. But the others had already cut the hobbles to their horses and were pulling them away.

Longarm finally reached the shore and snatched up a Winchester. With water cascading off his bare body, he plunged into the brush and did not go ten feet before he stepped on stickers and sharp stones that sent him howling to his knees with pain. By the time he was able to get back to his feet, the horses and the Indians were gone.

"Custis!" Lilly cried. "Custis did you get our horses?"

"No!"

He heard Lilly wail in consternation, then cry, "We're doomed!"

Limping painfully back to the beach where they'd planned to camp, Longarm collapsed beside the water and turned the tender soles of his feet up to where he could give them a proper inspection. His feet were lacerated and many of the terrible thorns he'd picked up still protruded from his flesh.

"Oh man," he growled, "I've got to get these pulled

out, or my feet will surely get infected. Lilly, come over here and give me a hand!"

Lilly was frantically trying to get dressed. "Your feet will have to wait," she snapped, levering a shell into the breech of her rifle. "I'm going after those horses!"

"If you leave here without me they'll probably set a trap and either take you as a hostage to sell to the Apache . . . or else kill you."

"Maybe," she replied, "but, if I wait until we pull all those stickers from the soles of your feet, we'll never see our horses again and we'll die by this river."

"No, we won't," he said, starting to use the nails of his thumb and second finger to pinch and pull out the thorns. "Because Topoki can't be more than another eight or ten miles from us, and we can't get lost if we follow this river."

For a long moment, Lilly seemed to hang in the balance of indecision. Finally, she nodded her head and flopped down beside him, her face, arms and legs streaked with mud. "How could we let something like this happen?"

"They were probably watching and following us for miles," Longarm told her. "I expect they had planned to steal our horses and about everything else we own after we fell asleep. They might even have intended to slit our throats. So you see, things could be even worse."

"Not much," Lilly said, her anger boiling to the surface. "You're a lawman and a ranger. I thought you'd know enough to keep this kind of disaster from happening."

Longarm was feeling guilty enough without her scorn. "All right," he said shortly, "so I'm not perfect, and I made a simple mistake."

"Simple?" she mocked. "Do you call what happened here just a 'simple mistake'?"

"All right!" he yelled, pulling out a thorn buried at least a half inch into his poor foot and biting his lip to keep from wailing in pain, "so it was a major mistake. Does my saying it make you happy?"

"Nothing could possibly make me happy right now,"

she told him. "I lost my horse, and I'm about to die of the heat. I don't see how we could get into a worse fix."

"Believe me," he told her. "Things can get a lot worse than they are right now."

"How?"

"Well," Longarm said, steeling himself to yank out another deep thorn, "what if those fellas that stole our horses have a whole bunch of friends camped nearby? Do you think maybe they might come back to finish us off, and take what they didn't get the first time?"

Lilly's eyes widened as she saw his point. "Oh my . . . let's get those thorns out of your feet and get out of here!"

Longarm thought that was an excellent idea. And even though he could put on his stockings and boots, he knew that it was going to hurt like the devil to walk the rest of the way to Topoki.

The alternative, however, left little doubt that walking was their best and only hope.

Chapter 10

They didn't say much that night as they trudged the long, difficult miles on to Topoki. More than once Longarm and Lilly heard the rattle of a snake in the weeds, causing them to detour around in the darkness, often falling into the mud. They finally arrived at Topoki around two o'clock in the morning. The village was dark and Longarm observed nothing but a saloon, a livery and five or six huts. He reckoned that Topoki was about as humble a place as you'd ever want to avoid.

"I can't believe that anyone would choose to live here," Lilly said as she gazed downriver at the sorry collection of buildings. "But this is where Monty told me his sister-in-law came with Tyler."

"How long ago?" Custis asked, undressing and wading into the river to cool down because the temperature was still in the mid-nineties.

"A couple of years."

"Did you ever meet her?"

"No."

Longarm collapsed in the river, sloshing water over his head. He was tired, depressed and very much doubted if he would find Tyler still living in this miserable Mohave hellhole.

"What was Henrietta's sister's name?" he asked when Lilly sank down in the water beside him.

"Daisy."

"Last name?"

"I have no idea."

"Great," Longarm said peevishly. "We've come all the way out here to find a kid we've never seen living with a woman we've never seen and whose last name we don't even know. How are we even supposed to . . . Oh, never mind."

The river gurgled softly and night birds called from the swampy inlets along the shore. Longarm leaned back and gazed up at the stars. At least the night sky was familiar. Otherwise, he might just as well have been on another planet for all the similarity there was between Topoki and Denver.

"So how do you like the adventure of traveling we're having so far?" he asked.

"Oh shut up," she said wearily. "I wasn't thinking of this kind of thing when I pictured us traveling. You know that."

"Yeah," he said, feeling a little guilty for being so sarcastic. "I know. But at least we can be pretty well assured that things can't get much worse."

"Can we?"

"I think so."

Lilly splashed water over her head. She looked terrible and her voice was filled with weariness when she asked, "What are we going to do if Daisy has disappeared?"

"It's not Daisy I'm after. I just want to find Tyler and make sure that he knows about his father and that he's doing all right."

"And what if he isn't?"

Longarm had given that some thought. "I'm not much good with kids," he admitted. "But Tyler will be about thirteen. Seems to me that the least I can do is take him back with me to Denver and see that he gets a good foster home and an education. Maybe I can even help him in other ways."

"Like teach him how to handle a gun and shoot bad men?"

Longarm laughed out loud. "You're feeling damned near as ornery as I am this morning. Maybe we ought to scoot back on shore and try to catch a few winks before the sun comes up."

"Not me," she said. "Not with those Indians lurking around in the bushes. And what are we going to do about our stolen horses?"

"I don't know," Longarm admitted. "By now, the Indians have probably found our saddles that were too heavy for us to carry. So I guess that just leaves us with what we brought this far. How much money do you have in your traveling bag?"

"None of your business."

"I expect that it is my business," Longarm said, standing up in the water and going over to their baggage. He opened one of Lilly's traveling bags before she could stop him and was amazed to see that it was stuffed with cash. "My . . . oh . . . my!"

"Give me that!"

Longarm handed her the bag and the money. "Looks like we're better off than I thought we were. With that much cash, you could buy us a stagecoach and a team of matched horses."

"But I won't."

"Then a couple of replacement mounts will do."

Lilly just snorted, so Longarm sat down on the beach and gathered up his weapons. He patted her on her wet, muddy thigh and said, "Cheer up! Things always look brighter in the morning."

"Not here," she said morosely. "Here things will only be hotter."

Longarm stretched out in the cool mud with water up to his chest and with little more than his head resting on the riverbank. "I'm going to sleep until morning. Don't let the Indians, the scorpions or the gila monsters get us before the Indians come around."

"What are gila monsters?"

"They're big, fat lizards about a yard long and six inches wide. They're kind of colorful but mighty poisonous."

"Will they attack humans?"

"Only at night."

Lilly wailed, but Longarm closed his eyes and let the lullaby of the river put him to sleep.

"Wake up," she insisted, splashing water in his face.

Longarm started into consciousness and rolled over in the shallows. He saw Lilly standing out deeper in the river trying to wash the mud off of herself and prepare for their arrival in Topoki. Longarm yawned and would have paid a dollar for a pot of coffee. But there wouldn't be any coffee until he got to the saloon or one of the houses, and so he waded out to join Lilly and scrub himself off as best as he could. The sun was well up, and it was probably seven o'clock in the morning, but nothing was moving yet in the nearby village.

When they waded out and got fully dressed, they gathered their weapons and baggage and walked into the settlement. Several dogs came out to bark at them, but no one appeared.

"I got a feeling that not much happens around here," Longarm said as he and Lilly stood in the center of the village waiting for someone to show their face.

"I have the same feeling."

Longarm smelled coffee and followed the scent toward the saloon. "Let's go knock on the door, and see if we can get some breakfast."

"I'm not buying it for the both of us," Lilly warned.

"Now don't you be going stingy on me," Longarm told the woman. "If you're going to act that way, I'll just leave you right here."

Even though her face was dirty, Longarm could see that

the woman paled with alarm. "You wouldn't."

"Don't try me. Anything I hate is a tightwad and a miser. You've got plenty of money to get us out of this fix, so don't be afraid to use it."

"But I wanted to spend it on us traveling to San Francisco and then to Seattle!"

"How about let's just see if we can find Tyler and get out of this desert," he suggested.

Lilly nodded and followed Custis up to the door of the saloon. He knocked and then pushed the door open and walked inside. The saloon wasn't much, but it did have a roof and walls. The floor was covered with flat rocks and the cracks between them were filled with sand and gravel. There was a long bar made of a half-sawed log that must have come from some distant mountains after having been floated down the river. There were glasses behind the bar along with a small man with bat ears and a stovepipe hat who was drinking coffee.

"Morning," the bartender said without much enthusiasm. "Gonna be another pisser out there today."

"Sure is," Longarm said. "We had our horses stolen, and we sure could use some coffee and breakfast."

The man studied Longarm, then Lilly several moments before he said, "If you've got cash, I've got coffee, and I can fry you up some pork and make some sourdough biscuits. Cost you a dollar each . . . and that includes the coffee and all you can eat."

"You've got a deal," Longarm said.

The man poured them coffee and brought it over to a poker table where Longarm and Lilly took their seats. He got a real good look at Lilly and said, "Don't take offense, miss, but you're lookin' a little gritty."

"That's because I am gritty. I'm as dirty as a sow and mad as a teased snake, so don't give me any of your lip, buster."

"No ma'am!" he said, retreating back behind his bar. "Maybe after you've had something to eat, you'd like to

97

take a bath. Only cost you four bits and that includes the soap."

"I'll do it," she told him.

They drank their coffee and had little to say as the man disappeared into a back room. Very soon, however, they could smell the pork and baking biscuits. Longarm helped himself to the coffee pot. "If it is true . . . as some say . . . that the Colorado River is too thick to pour and too thin to slice, then I'd have to judge that this coffee is mostly river water."

"Why didn't you ask about Tyler?"

"Because I wanted to enjoy my breakfast before I get any more bad news."

"Oh."

When their breakfast arrived, the bartender insisted on being paid before he gave them their plates. But the food was surprisingly good, and both Longarm and Lilly ate enough to get their money's worth. When they were finished, Longarm asked, "You have cigars for sale?"

"I do. Cost two bits each."

"Are they from Cuba?"

"No, Mexico."

Longarm groaned, but he bought one of the short, black cigars and poured the last of the coffee into his cup. He lit the cigar and nearly broke into a coughing fit, then asked, "Do you know of a woman named Daisy that lived here with a boy named Tyler?"

"Yeah, I remember them."

"Meaning they are gone?"

"Sure," the bartender said. "Why would any woman in her right mind stay here unless it was to . . ." He looked at Lilly and said, "Well, unless it was to commit sin."

"How long ago did she and the boy leave?"

The man thumbed back his stovepipe hat and considered the question very carefully. "Let's see. It was the spring that the Colorado flooded the worst it has since I arrived eight years ago. And that was . . . well, it was about five years ago. Yes, sir, the woman and the boy left five years ago last spring."

"Any idea where they went?"

"I sure do."

Longarm waited, but no answer was forthcoming. And since he was not an overly patient man, he growled, "Where, dammit?"

"Hmmm," the bartender mused. "My memory always serves me better when I've had a whiskey."

"Then pour yourself one! You're the bartender, aren't you?"

"Yes, but also the owner, and I can't pay myself to drink my own whiskey."

"Meaning you expect me to buy you a drink before you'll tell me where they went?"

"That would help grease the mind a mite."

Longarm jumped up and grabbed the man by the throat. "I'm tired of you trying to weasel every cent you can out of us, mister. Now you tell me where they went and be quick about it! If you lie to me, I'll come back and burn you and this place to the ground."

The bartender's face turned purple and he choked, "All right! All right! They're still living down at Yuma!"

"Are you sure?" Longarm released his grip, so the man could elaborate.

"Sure I'm sure! The woman ran off and left the kid. Tyler is a deck hand working on a paddle wheeler that comes upriver every two weeks with mail, liquor and my supplies."

"He can't be more than thirteen."

"Around here, that's old enough to do a man's work."

"When is the paddle wheeler coming next?"

"It'll be here in two weeks."

"You mean it just left?"

"That's right," the man said. "It was here only yesterday."

"Damn the luck!" Longarm frowned. "Is there any

other regularly scheduled passenger boats coming and going?"

"There's a barge that they pole up and down this river. They use Indians to push it upriver, and it just floats back down. It carries some passengers and supplies."

"When is it going to Yuma?"

The bartender replied, "I expect it to come by any day now."

"Good! Then we'll board it, and float on down to Yuma to find the boy."

"I got rooms upstairs that I'll rent to you for two dollars a day."

"One dollar for the both of us, and I'm in no mood to argue," Longarm told the man.

"Okay."

When the barge appeared the next afternoon, it was even cruder than Longarm had expected. It was about thirty feet long and little more than some logs bound together with rope. There was a tiller on the back and about five thin Yuma Indians sitting or sleeping on the stern. They were, Longarm decided, the pushers who were now taking their ease as the barge floated downriver with the steady but slow current.

The owner of the barge was a man named Ira Blake, and he was taciturn and as dirty and sullen as the Indians he hired.

"Five dollars each to Yuma," was all he said as he stuck out his filthy hand for their money.

"How many days to Yuma?" Longarm asked.

"Two or three."

"Make it two and we'll pay you double," Lilly told the man.

"Might do that."

So they left Topoki without a backward glance and headed on down the muddy river. There sure wasn't much to see. Just a wild burro or two and an occasional coyote and bighorn sheep. Blake tried to shoot the sheep for meat, but missed every time because he never stopped pulling on a big jug of corn liquor.

Longarm removed most of his clothing and spent a lot of time swimming in the Colorado trying to keep from frying on the unshaded barge as it floated along at a snail's pace.

"Why don't you pay those Indians to use their poles so that we could get to Yuma faster?" Lilly finally demanded. "This sun is burning us to a crisp!"

Blake was as dark as a Mexican. He had a full beard and a big hat, and he didn't like getting advice from anyone—especially a woman. But after Lilly pestered him for a few hours about getting the Yuma Indians to pole the barge so they could go faster, Blake finally lost patience and said, "The Indians wouldn't do it for any amount of money."

"Why?"

"Because they would think it stupid to work at something that didn't need to be worked at because we're runnin' with this river. And I think you're stupid for not seein' that fact yourself."

Longarm thought Lilly was going to snatch Blake's jug from his hands and bash it over his head, but she didn't. Instead, she dove into the river and swam until she cooled down. He also noticed that the Indians liked to watch Lilly swim because her clothes clung to her body and they could see her long white legs.

Chapter 11

They floated all afternoon, many times running aground on sand and mud bars. Whenever that happened, Blake shouted at the sullen Indians, who would climb to their feet, reluctantly take their poles and then push the barge free. Sometimes, however, they would be stuck so firmly that the Indians would have to jump over the sides and swim around and under the barge, grunting and heaving until their heavy vessel finally broke loose from the thick mud and resumed its slow journey south down the Colorado.

"How come you let that happen so often?" Lilly complained. "What kind of a river boat captain are you?"

"I'm no 'river boat captain' " Blake said, his words slurred from the whiskey. "I'm a river rat stuck on this stinking water with a bunch of damned Indians that don't want to work but sure like to get paid."

His answer didn't satisfy Lilly. "That doesn't excuse the fact that we seem to be wasting more time getting ourselves unstuck from the mud than we do floating."

Blake's dark eyes sparked with intense dislike. "Woman," he growled, "this river changes every day. The deep currents move in circles and that pushes the bars around so that you can't tell where they'll be from one hour to the next. So don't be givin' me a bad time or else you can have your money back and walk all the way down to Yuma!"

"She isn't walking anywhere," Longarm said, trying to keep the peace. Blake muttered an oath under his breath then glared at Longarm and said, "Best thing you two could do is to jump overboard and hang on to the sides so this barge is lighter."

Lilly was furious. "We paid your price to ride on this miserable collection of rotting logs. Now why don't you just stop pulling on that jug of whiskey and do a better job of navigating?"

Ira Blake wasn't a man accustomed to being talked back to by anyone, and when his hand went to the gun on his hip, Longarm was sure that he would have shot Lilly dead if he hadn't intervened. "Blake, don't even think about pulling that gun!"

The boatman turned on him, but when he saw that Longarm's own hand was resting on the butt of his gun, he was sober enough to back down. "Damn passengers ain't worth the bother," he muttered, taking another pull from his jug, but finding it empty.

"Damn," he muttered, reaching under a tarp for a refill and placing the empty beside a half dozen other jugs.

Just before sundown, the current pushed them far up onto a long island of mud and Blake loudly cursed their poor luck. He jumped off the barge yelling at his Indians to give him a helping hand in the water. While Longarm and Lilly sat and watched from above, Blake and his Yuma Indians heaved and strained. But, despite their best efforts, the barge would not budge.

Blake glared up at them with angry, bloodshot eyes. "Don't just stand there watching us . . . get into the river and help!"

"I guess we'd better do as the man says," Longarm told Lilly. "Our weight might make the difference."

"I don't believe this," she said bitterly. "We'd have been better off walking."

"We tried that. Remember?"

Longarm took Lilly's arm and they jumped into the shallow water. Blake was cursing the Indians and giving orders that they all should put their shoulders to the task and lift in unison. The logs were waterlogged and the barge was heavy but, after several tries, Longarm could feel it breaking free of the clinging black mud.

"Indians!" Blake shouted. "Back on board and grab your poles. Then push! Give it everything you have, now!"

The Yumas clambered back onto the barge and were soon straining on the ends of their stout poles. Between their efforts on board and that of Longarm and Lilly in the water, the barge broke free.

"Thank heavens," Lilly said, panting and gasping in the hot, humid air as the barge again floated.

Longarm was also shaking from exhaustion. He had planted his bare feet deep into the mud and used every ounce of his strength. Now, he wanted nothing more than to crawl back on the barge and lie still while he caught his breath.

"See you later, suckers!"

Longarm glanced up to see Blake with a gun clenched in his fist and pointed at his head. The boatman wore a devilish smile, and there wasn't a doubt in Longarm's mind that the man would shoot both him and Lilly if they protested or offered threats.

"Are you going to let him leave us here?" Lilly cried, starting to wade through the mud toward the barge.

Longarm grabbed and held the distraught woman. "Listen to me," he hissed, hugging her tight and pressing his lips to her ear. "Just sink down in the water and don't say a word. Blake is drunk and crazy enough to fill us full of holes right where we stand. Don't provoke the man or we're dead."

Lilly covered her face with her hands and cried, "But everything we have is on that barge. My money. Everything."

"We'll get it back," Longarm promised. "The important thing right now is just to stay alive."

"But . . ."

Longarm clamped his hand over Lilly's mouth and pulled her down into the water where they sat and watched as Blake roared with insane laughter. The Indians also seemed to think the situation was very funny. And so, as the barge resumed its slow progress down the river, and the Indians poled out into a deeper channel, Longarm and Lilly had no choice but to watch it disappear around a bend.

"Is this never going to end?" Lilly wailed. "First, the Indians steal our horses, and now, this horrible man takes whatever else we had left. Custis, we aren't getting out of this wilderness alive. Without weapons or horses, we'll die on this river!"

"No, we won't," Longarm grated, burning with the heat and his anger. "And I guarantee you that we'll recover everything we've just lost and that I'll make Ira Blake wish he'd never been born. But first, we have to survive until we reach Yuma or someone else comes floating downriver to give us some help."

Lilly turned her head up toward the empty river, and there were tears in her eyes when she asked, "Do you think anyone else might be coming along soon?"

"I have no idea. But we can't count on that possibility. We have to do the best that we can to reach Yuma."

"Custis, we aren't even wearing shoes! The sharp rocks and thorns along the riverbank will cut our feet to ribbons."

"You're right," Longarm agreed. "So we'd better find a log and start floating."

Before Lilly could reply, Longarm spied a dead cottonwood lying half in and half out of the water. There were many such trees and he wasted no time in swimming over to the tree and breaking off a thick limb about six feet long.

"This will do just fine," he said, trying, but failing, to

sound optimistic. "Let's wade back out in the swiftest part of the river and get going. If we put some effort into it, we might even overtake Blake and his barge sometime tonight."

"If we do, we can drown him like the river rat he is!" Lilly hissed.

"I doubt we can do that."

"Why not? He's drunk and bent on getting even drunker."

"Sure," Longarm said, "but the Yuma Indians are sober, and I don't think they'd take kindly to us killing their employer. No, Lilly, the best we can hope for is to catch them all by surprise and somehow get to our weapons before they know what is happening."

Lilly glanced up the sun. "We've got maybe two hours left of daylight. My skin is already burned and wrinkled up like a dried prune."

"Here," Longarm said, removing his shirt and tying it like a turban around her head so that it was low on her brow and just barely above the woman's eyes.

"Thanks," Lilly told him. "But what about you? Your hat is on that barge with your boots."

Longarm was still wearing his pants. He removed them and fashioned another turbanlike affair on his head. It was cumbersome and heavy with water yet far better than nothing.

"You look ridiculous!" Lilly said, managing a smile.

"I know, but so do you," Longarm told her as he grabbed the limb and started pushing it out into the river. "Let's stop the chatter and get to work. Maybe Blake and his Indians plan to stop and sleep for a while. If they do that, we might just be able to sneak up and get our guns before they awaken."

"I can't imagine sneaking past Indians," Lilly said as the water got deep enough that they had to leave their footing and begin to swim, kicking at the sluggish current.

After an hour, their legs grew so heavy that it was impossible to kick anymore, so they just clung to the limb and tried to keep it in the deepest part of the river. But their efforts often failed and brought them onto a sand or mud bar. With only a limb to free, it took just moments to move back out into deep water and continue.

"At the rate we're going," Longarm said, "we ought to soon overtake Blake and his boys."

"If we do that in daylight," she replied, "he'll try to shoot us like fish in a barrel."

"You're right," Longarm told her. "So we might as well take our time until after it gets dark."

"I think," Lilly said, "we ought to just stay back and try to reach Yuma. Once we get there, you can show your badge to the authorities and arm yourself. Then, we can find and fix that damned Ira Blake once and for all."

"I can't show my badge," Longarm said. "It's resting in one of my vest pockets."

"Oh that's good," she said cryptically. "So even if we do reach Yuma, you can't really use your authority because you have no proof of who you are."

"That's not true," Longarm said, his voice quiet but filled with resolve. "When we get to Yuma, I'll take charge . . . with or without a badge. We'll find both Ira Blake and young Kilpatrick."

"I sure hope so," Lilly said, resting her chin on the limb as they floated along. "I just want my money back, and then I want to leave because I am fed up with this hellish desert."

"Can't say that I'm having that much fun either," Longarm told her, blinking tears from his eyes because the glare of the setting sun off the moving river water was almost blinding.

Chapter 12

Night settled over the Colorado River like a warm blessing. Waterfowl silently glided to rest, taking refuge in the small inlets and thick marshes while the deep, throaty roar of bullfrogs filled the air along both banks of the great river.

A short time earlier, Lilly had complained of cramping leg muscles, so they had gone to shore where Longarm had massaged her thighs and calves until the pain subsided. The stars appeared one by one until the heavens were glittering and the moon lifted over a barren mountain top. The lonesome call of coyotes joined in chorus with the croaking of the bullfrogs, and now and then, they heard the sharp, almost eerie screech of an owl or some other large, night hunting bird.

"We'd better get moving again," Longarm decided aloud. "With luck, we'll either overtake the barge tonight, or, at worst, we'll float up to Yuma before this time tomorrow night."

"I know," Lilly told him. "But I'm so tired I could die."

"You *will* die if we don't get back in the water and float along," he said. "Without weapons, we're at the mercy of anyone who chances upon us, and that would most likely be more Yuma Indians. However, it could also be Mohaves, which I understand are not known for their hospitality to white people."

"All right," she said, eyes sunken and face drawn and haggard. "But I'm sure tired of that river."

"It's what's keeping us alive for the time being," Longarm told her as he gently helped her back into the Colorado.

"If you say so," she answered, not sounding very encouraged.

Longarm wasn't feeling much like going back into the water either, but he sure didn't see much future for them hanging around on the banks of a nearly deserted river. So they waded out until the water reached Lilly's neck and then pushed off into the current.

"Aren't you wishing you'd stayed up on your cattle ranch?" he asked after they'd floated for awhile.

"Yeah," she agreed. "At least right now I am. What about you?"

"Oh, this isn't so terrible," he mused, gently kicking at the water as they glided down the Colorado, "I've been in a whole lot worse messes."

"That's hard for me to imagine."

"Heck, Lilly. I've been shot, stabbed and whacked over the head with an axe handle, the butt of a pistol and even a silver-headed cane. I've been kicked and once a fella that got me in a fix even tried to pour kerosene on my head and make me into a flaming torch."

"That's amazing. Custis, for the life of me I don't know why you stick with this line of work," she said, gazing up at the moon. "And I'll bet it doesn't even pay very much."

"Nope. But the job does have its moments."

"Like when?"

"Like *now*."

Her head snapped down and she stared at him. "Now?" she asked, not bothering to hide her disbelief.

"Sure," Longarm confessed. "You see, it's my belief that most people go through their whole lives in kind of a state of perpetual boredom. Me, I go out on these cases, and I'm never bored. Sometimes I'm sort of defeated . . . like right now. But then I tell myself not to give up or get too discouraged, and things will turn out okay."

"I admire your attitude . . . if not your sense."

"Look at this as a learning experience," Longarm explained.

"Learning what?"

"Well, for example, I've learned never to leave my gun and boots out of reach when I'm around a man that I don't know or trust with my life. I should have been more careful, but the water felt so good, and we were stuck, so I let my guard down and learned a hard lesson."

"That's one way of looking at this predicament."

"It'll work out," Longarm promised.

"I sure hope so," Lilly told him. "There was two thousand dollars in my luggage. Two thousand dollars! I doubt that I'll ever see that money again, and Wade will know I took it. So what am I to do but go back and beg him to forgive me for being such a fool and a runaway?"

"We'll get your money back if we can overtake the barge before Blake spends it all on liquor down in Yuma."

"Are you going to kill that man?"

"Not unless I have to," Longarm told her. "There's a big prison there, and I'll most likely arrest Blake and see that he gets sentenced to a long term in that hellhole. Actually, it's a far worse fate than death. The inmates live in these small brick and adobe cells, and it gets so hot it nearly boils their brains. The guards allow them just one afternoon a week to be herded down to the river where they can bathe, wash their clothes and cool down. Other than that, they spend the whole summer locked up in those cooking cells."

"It does sound like a fate worse than death," Lilly agreed. "How much farther do you think it is to Yuma?"

"Maybe ten miles. No more than thirty. I can't really be sure since I've never been down this river."

"I just wish we were already there," Lilly said wistfully.

"And then we could go on to San Francisco where it's always cool and where they say that the Pacific Ocean is as blue as a high mountain lake."

Longarm was about to reply when they lazily rounded a bend in the river and saw a campfire burning about a half mile to the south on the Arizona side.

"Who is it?" Lilly asked.

"I expect it's Ira Blake and his Yuma Indians."

"But why would they stop?"

"I don't know. Maybe Blake passed out from all the heat and whiskey."

"What are we going to do?"

"We'll push for the shore and then sneak down the riverbank and, if they're asleep, I'll try to get my gun," Longarm said.

"What if they're awake?"

"Then we wait until they either fall asleep or start off down the river again."

"Then we'll try to attack them?"

"Quit askin' so damned many questions. In situations like this, you have to make decisions as the circumstances change. I don't know exactly what is going to happen next. I find it best to just take things as they come."

"Fine for you, but I prefer a plan," she told him. "I've always figured things out in advance, and then they seem to work out better."

"Just be quiet and let's get to shore." He pointed across the water. "See that rocky point up ahead?"

"Yeah."

"Let's shoot for that as our landing. And don't talk anymore or splash when you kick. Sound carries a long way over water."

"Any more orders?"

"Just button your lips and keep your feet kicking underwater," he told her.

It took them less than five minutes to reach the point. At Longarm's insistence, they smeared their arms and faces with mud then stayed low and eased out of the water, wincing with pain as they stepped on sharp rocks and an occasional buried branch.

The frogs around them stopped croaking but Longarm hoped the Indians wouldn't notice because their noisy brethren up and down the river never let up with their loud chorus.

"Do you hear anything from their camp?" Lilly whispered.

"No. It's just up through those weeds."

"I sure hope we don't step on a rattlesnake." Lilly clung to his arm. "Because if one bites me, I'm going to scream loud enough to be heard back in Denver."

"It's unlikely that we'll step on a snake," Longarm told her, hoping it was true.

Finally, they saw the fire again through the tall marsh grass. Longarm eased down on his stomach, and Lilly did the same. They watched for several minutes and saw nothing that moved in the camp. The barge was tied by a rope to the rotting stump of a cottonwood and, just up on the bank, there were the dark forms of the sleeping Indians.

"I don't see Blake," Longarm whispered. "Do you?"

"There's something long lying on the barge that wasn't there before. It might be him."

Longarm spotted the dark silhouette. "You're right. It probably is Blake. No doubt he doesn't trust his Indians enough to sleep with them for fear they'd slit his throat and drink all his jugs of whiskey."

"So what are you going to do?"

Longarm gave that question a few moments of concentrated thought before he said, "I'm going back into the river. I'll ease up to the barge, slip on board and knock Blake out before he can sound the alarm. Then you swim over to the barge. We'll get it untied and ease out into the current. With luck, the Yumas will never awaken and we'll be miles down the river before they realize the barge is gone."

"All right," she said in a low but steady voice. "But, if

you get into trouble, don't expect me to do anything. I'll just drown myself."

"Whatever suits you," he said, backing toward the river.

Longarm returned to the water, and it was easy enough to let the current carry him around the point to where the barge was tied. He gripped the logs and, hoping that he could get on board without shifting the barge much, he heaved himself up and onto its deck. Ira Blake was snoring loudly and Longarm rose to his feet, then walked over to the man and saw a rifle lying by his side. Picking up the weapon, Longarm slammed the rifle's heavy butt down on Blake's forehead not really caring if he caved in the boatman's skull.

Blake grunted, expelled a deep, gaseous sigh that reeked of bad whiskey and lay still as a stone. Longarm reached down and felt for a pulse. He was almost disappointed to find one.

Moments later, he had his six-gun and his derringer along with his clothes gathered in a pile. He also had Lilly's bag of cash. Creeping up to the bow of the barge, he waved in the moonlight, and it didn't take Lilly but a few moments to join him.

Longarm untied the barge and then climbed into the water and pushed off until the current took the barge and sent it gliding down the river.

"We did it!" Lilly cried when they had rounded a bend a half mile below the campfire so that only the light of the moon and stars were visible. "We're free!"

"That's right, and Blake didn't have a chance to spend any of your precious money."

"*Our* money," she corrected.

"'Ours'?" he asked with surprise.

"Well, why not? You've redeemed yourself and saved not only our hides but the money. I'm a very grateful woman."

Longarm chuckled. "I told you that we'd have an adventure and loads of excitement."

"Did you kill him?" Lilly asked, gesturing toward Blake's body.

"No," Longarm said. "But I sure smashed him a good one in the head. I might even have damaged his brains."

"He didn't have any to begin with. Or, if he did, they'd soaked up his whiskey and gone to rot."

Longarm figured that was true enough. If Ira Blake was still alive when they reached Yuma, they'd need to find a wagon to haul him up to the prison where he'd be tossed into a baking cell. If he survived the first few days, maybe the Yuma heat would eventually bake the booze out of his brains.

"Come here," Lilly said, stripping off her wet and muddy clothes. "Sometimes money isn't enough reward."

Longarm was caught off guard. "Do you want to make love right now?"

"Why not?" she asked. "There's a big moon out tonight and given all the adventure we seem to be having, who knows what will happen tomorrow?"

He shucked out of his own wet clothing. "Sure," he said, reaching for her and a blanket, so they didn't scratch up their backsides on the rough deck. "Why not?"

Longarm mounted Lilly on the barge and they went at it like a couple of lust-crazed beavers. When they were finally finished, they sampled some of Ira Blake's whiskey. It was terrible, just as they'd expected it to be, but the night was still young and the golden moonlight melted across the rolling river make them feel giddy, almost like kids that were playing hooky from school.

"I got a feeling we're going to have a real good time before we reach Yuma," he said, handing her the jug and already feeling the powerful corn liquor in his veins.

"Yuma?" she giggled. "Who cares about Yuma until the damn hot sun comes up tomorrow morning. Right now we've got everything anyone could ask for . . . and more."

Longarm ran his hands over her firm buttocks and then up to caress her breasts. "You're right about that," he replied. "Let's go for a swim and then drink some more of this moonshine."

They both dived into the water and swam around the barge as happy and playful as a couple of river otters. Longarm felt good and strong, and when he saw Lilly's naked bottom porpoise in the water, he felt like he wanted to sample something a lot more exciting than Ira Blake's strong moonshine. So he swam after Lilly just to see if they could do it in the water.

Chapter 13

They arrived in Yuma the next afternoon without further
incident. Blake had regained consciousness which made
it all the easier to drag him off the barge and then hire a
buckboard to deliver him to the prison which stood grim
and imposing over the Colorado. The prison was a log
stockade with guard towers at the corners so that it had a
commanding view of the river and the village at Yuma
Crossing, which was located mostly on the California
side. In its brief but violent history, only three men had
even dared try to escape the Yuma Prison, and all of them
had been shot before even managing to reach the river.

"This man robbed and then abandoned us upriver,"
Longarm told the warden after Blake had been locked in
a dungeonlike cell. "He also tried to kill us."

Warden Cotton was a tall, officious-looking man who
brooked no nonsense from anyone. He didn't ask for par-
ticulars but said, "We know Ira Blake well. He's a scoun-
drel, and he's been here twice before, although only for
public drunkenness and fighting. But this time I reckon
we can give him a good dose of Arizona justice. Who is
the lady traveling with you?"

"Her name is Lilly. She comes from up around Flagstaff."

"Wish I were up there right now," Cotton said, using his handkerchief to wipe his brow. "It was almost a hundred and twenty degrees yesterday and it's every bit as hot today."

"It's a pisser, all right," Longarm said in agreement.

The warden asked, "Where you from, Marshal?"

"Denver."

"Well, if you don't mind my saying so, you and the lady both look like you've been dragged through hell."

Longarm rubbed his stubbled beard. "Warden, that pretty well describes it."

"What are you doing way down here in the low country?"

"I'm looking for a young man named Tyler Kilpatrick."

The warden frowned and thought for a moment, but then said, "Can't say as I've heard of him. How old would he be?"

"Only about thirteen. His father was the marshal up in Mountain City. He saved my life once and wrote me a letter asking me to look after his son, but he hadn't seen the boy in many years because his wife took the kid and ran away."

"Why didn't your friend track her down?"

"I don't know," Longarm answered. "But I understand from Lilly that the kid was taken to Topoki and then he and the kid's aunt named Daisy moved down here to Yuma about five years ago. The bartender in Topoki said Tyler was working on a barge as a deckhand, but I'm not sure that he knew what he was talking about."

"Hmmm," the warden mused aloud. "There is a young fella named TK that works on Milo Jarvin's paddle-wheel steamer. But TK sure looks older than thirteen. Of course, he might just be big for his age, and the hard river work would age a young fella fast."

"Where can I find him?"

"Follow me," the warden said.

Longarm's heart sank. "You mean Tyler is locked up here in your prison?"

"No. But we'll walk up to the guard tower and be able to look across the river. If Jarvin's paddle wheel is tied up there waitin' to be loaded or unloaded, then you can be sure that the TK is close by."

Longarm grabbed Lilly's arm as they all marched across the prison grounds and then mounted a series of stairs that brought them up to the covered guard tower where a lone rifleman was sitting and smoking a cigarette. He jumped to his feet as soon as he saw he had visitors and loudly announced, "Just takin' a little break, Warden. All is quiet up here. Mighty hot, though."

"It's gonna get even hotter up here if you don't stay off your butt and keep your eyes on the lookout like you're getting paid to do!"

"Yes, sir!" The guard hurried to the edge of his tower and began looking up and down the river as if he were expecting the Second Coming of Jesus.

Cotton gave the man a withering look of disgust and said something about how you couldn't find any good employees anymore. Then, he laid his elbows on the log railing and stared across the muddy river. "Yep," he said after a few moments. "That's Milo's boat all right, and I'd say it was loaded and about ready to get up a full head of steam."

"Which one?"

Cotton pointed it out. "See the little boiler? It's blowin' a fine plume of steam which means it's about ready to head upriver."

Longarm had come too far to let Monty's son slip away from him, so he grabbed Lilly as he took the stairs two at a time and yelled over his shoulder, "Thanks, Warden!"

"Don't mention it! But watch out for Milo. He's a rough and tough son of a bitch and he won't like you taking one of his deck hands . . . if that's your intention."

Longarm didn't give a tinker's damn what Milo liked or didn't like. He'd sworn to find and help Tyler Kilpatrick, and if he and TK were one and the same, then Longarm would fulfill his promise.

"Slow down!" Lilly cried as Longarm dragged her out of the prison and they headed toward the river. "My feet are killing me, and it's way too hot to hurry."

"Then wait here for me, because I'm not about to let that paddle wheeler get out of sight!"

Longarm ran the rest of the way down to the river and unbuckled his gunbelt. He was kicking off his boots and tearing off his shirt when Lilly caught up with him shouting, "Custis, are you crazy?"

"The paddle wheeler is starting to back out of its dock!" Longarm yelled a moment before diving into the water and swimming hard. "Watch over my gun and belongings!"

The current was swift, but Longarm was a good swimmer and he took what he figured was a proper angle, keeping an eye on the paddle wheeler. In the middle of the river, he felt a strong undercurrent trying to pull him down and, had he not been such a powerful swimmer, he would no doubt have drowned.

By now, riverboat captain Milo Jarvin was reversing his paddle wheels and the steamer was out in the deep central channel and just beginning to fight the current as it took on a full head of steam.

Suddenly, Longarm realized that the river was carrying him too fast toward the bow of the paddle wheeler and that, if he missed his grab, he stood an excellent chance of being run down and then beaten to pieces by the vessel's thrashing paddles.

Several of the paddle wheeler's deckhands saw Longarm and began to shout and wave him off, but Longarm wouldn't swim away as the bow of the surging paddle wheeler loomed closer and closer.

"I'm not moving!" he shouted. "Shut her down!"

But Milo Jarvin had no intention of doing anything of the sort. He was an experienced riverboat captain and he knew that, if he lost a full head of steam in this fast part of the channel, his boat would be swept downriver and run aground.

"Move outta the way, you drunken fool!" a deeply tanned deckhand shouted, his voice barely audible over the loud crashing of the paddles striking water and the shrill shriek of a steam whistle. "Turn and swim for your life!"

Instead, Longarm focused on a mooring rope hanging off the port side, and he swam toward it with every intention of grabbing the rope and then hauling himself on deck.

He swam hard with all his might and reached high for the rope but missed! He was struck by the surging bow of the paddle wheeler and almost knocked unconscious. Dazed and disoriented, he would have been pulled under except that a slender deckhand dove overboard and almost landed on him as he floundered.

"Dive!" the man shouted, then vanished swimming downward as the paddles churned almost on top of them.

Longarm understood. The current was too powerful to swim far enough away from the paddles, so he took a deep breath and dove, feeling caught in a maelstrom of churning water. He struck the gravelly bottom, lost and disoriented in the whirling mud, and felt the huge paddles pass overhead. Then, kicking off the bottom, he swam hard for the surface. Lungs on fire, he burst into sunlight and saw the young man close by.

"You crazy fool! What were you doing? Trying to kill yourself and me, too!"

The kid bore a strong resemblance to Monty Kilpatrick, and as they slowly swam for the Arizona shore which was closest, Longarm gasped and blurted, "Are you TK?"

"So what if I am?"

Longarm was struggling to catch his breath. "I'm . . . I'm Marshal Custis Long!"

Longarm would have explained things in greater detail, but the paddle wheeler was blasting its whistle, and he was too winded to say anything more until they touched river bottom a quarter of a mile below the Yuma Prison walls.

"Dammit!" TK wailed, "now I've missed the boat, and Milo ain't gonna risk trying to turn in the channel and get caught on a sandbar. What am I going to do now?"

Longarm slogged over to the shore where Lilly was waiting with a look of amazement on her face. "Custis, you nearly got yourself run over and drowned," she told him. "That was one of the stupidest things I've ever seen in my life."

"That's what I told him," TK said, hauling his skinny body out of the water and glaring at Custis. "And now I'm out of a damned job with no money saved! I should have let that fool get hisself drowned. That's what I should have done, all right!"

TK sounded angry, dejected and just plain disgusted with the man whose life he'd probably saved. "I should have minded my own business, and then I'd still have a job."

Longarm had heard enough. "Listen, kid. I came all the way from Denver to find you. I was your father's best friend. He asked me to take care of you."

TK just stared at Longarm. "I don't know what you're talkin' about, mister. You surely are crazy!"

"No, I'm not." He turned to Lilly, still sucking for air, and managed to say, "You talk to him."

"Me?"

"Yeah."

Lilly put her hands on her hips. "Custis Long is a United States marshal come all the way from Denver, Colorado to find you. I knew your mother, Henrietta. Your father, Monty Kilpatrick, was marshal of Mountain City. He was a good man and your mother shouldn't have run away, taking you from him."

"My father died!" TK shouted. "He died of the fever just after I was born."

Lilly wagged her head back and forth. "That's not true, Tyler."

"How'd you know my name?" the kid demanded.

"Because I knew your mother, and I knew of her sister,

122

Daisy. I helped Marshal Custis Long find you."

Tyler glared at Custis. "None of this is making any sense. I came here five years ago, and I been on my own pretty much since then. I don't need you or her or anyone. I have. . . . I *had* a job until you tried to drown yourself just now."

The kid watched the paddle wheeler continue upriver until it rounded a bend and was gone. "I guess I'll find me another job," he muttered, wading back into the water and preparing to swim across to the California side, where there were other barges and boats moored at the docks.

"Wait a minute," Longarm said, grabbing his arm. "I promised your father that I'd find you."

"My father didn't know me," Tyler spat. "He died when I was less than a year old and . . ."

Longarm had fumbled in his pocket and he brought out the letter that he'd been sent. "This was written by your father, Marshal Kilpatrick. You can see from the date that it was written less than three months ago. He didn't know where your mother had taken you. And he was too ashamed to come looking, because he figured maybe it was all his fault that your mother ran away with another man and took you with her."

Tyler's eyes blazed, and he shook his head. "I don't believe any of this. You did a crazy thing out in the river, and you're talking crazy right now, and I mean to get away from you."

"Can't you read?" Lilly asked.

Tyler swung toward her, eyes blazing. "So what if I can't? I was doin' just fine 'til you two crazies showed up. I don't need to learn no readin' and writin' to know that you're a couple of fools."

"We're not," Longarm said, buckling on his gunbelt and giving Tyler a good look at his badge. "And you're coming with me, even if I have to arrest you."

"Arrest me for what?"

"I'll think of something."

"You can't do that!"

"Watch me," Longarm said, realizing that he was going to have to be tough with Tyler, or the kid was going to get away.

Tyler shook his head, but the glint of a rifle barrel caught his eye from the guard's watchtower. "You wouldn't send me to that prison, would you?"

"I might," Longarm replied. "I just delivered a man up there named Ira Blake, and he's going to rot in a cell a long, long time."

"I know Ira. What'd Ira do now?"

"He went against me, and so he'll face a long prison term."

"What do you mean, 'He went against me'?"

Longarm chose his words carefully. "I gave him orders and he gave me grief . . . just like you're doing."

"So he went to prison for *that*?"

Longarm could see that Tyler was starting to take him seriously. "That's right. You want to go up and join him?"

"No, sir! I heard too many bad things about that place." Young Tyler was clearly shaken at the prospect of being imprisoned. "I don't want to go any nearer to it than I am right now."

"Then I think you had better do as I say."

"Meaning?"

"Meaning we've got some talking to do, and you're going to finally learn who your father was, and what kind of a man he was. And I got some things he left for you."

"My father left something for me?"

"A cabin in the mountains and some money . . . among other things."

Tyler's eyes went from Longarm to Lilly and back to Longarm again. He was finding this news hard to comprehend. "*I* got a cabin and some cash money?"

"And a lot to learn," Longarm said. "So are you willing to go have something to eat and then to start listening to what I have to say?"

"I believe I am," Tyler said. "Got nothing better to do now that I haven't got a job anymore."

"Good," Longarm told the kid. "Help the lady up the hill, and let's go find something to eat. We're starved, and you look like you haven't had a decent meal in months."

"I eat enough to get by," Tyler told them as they climbed the dry, rocky slope leading up to the sun-baked Yuma Prison.

Chapter 14

After telling young Kilpatrick all about his father over a huge meal of steaks, potatoes and slices of apple pie, Longarm and Lilly took Tyler shopping. They purchased new clothes, and, since Longarm's hat and boots had been ruined in the river, he bought replacements.

"So when can I go to Mountain City and see my father's place and the stuff he left me?" Tyler asked as they walked out into the street, realizing that night had fallen.

Longarm looked to Lilly. "Are you going back to the Rocking J or are you heading on to California?"

"I've been giving that a lot of thought."

"And?"

"I think I'll go back to the mountains and the ranch. Wade is probably worried sick, and I miss the smell of pines. I don't ever want to come back to this desert country again."

"It ain't that bad," Tyler said. "You sort of get used to the heat, and the river is always close, so you can jump in and cool off. Winters here are real nice."

"But this is still summer, and I can't take this heat," Lilly told him. "Custis, are you really going to Paradise?"

"If I can find it," he replied.

"I know where it is," Tyler said. "Been there once. It's

back up the river about eighty miles, then another fifty or so miles to the east."

"Sounds like it's still in the hot country."

"Paradise is higher, so it's a few degrees cooler."

"What's there?" Longarm wanted to know.

"It's gold, silver and copper mining country," the kid said. "They've had some big strikes up there, and there was another just a few months ago. I worked there for about a month, but then I saw a man killed in a mine cave-in, and so I quit."

"I thought that you were a riverboat man," Longarm said.

"Well," Tyler told him, stretching up to his full height and raising his chin proudly, "I go where I please when I please. And I can tell you this much . . . Paradise sure ain't no paradise. Whoever thought up the name for that town must have had a sick sense of humor."

"Pretty bad, huh?"

The kid looked at Longarm and said, "It's a tough town. And, if people there found out you were a United States marshal, you wouldn't last a day."

"Did you ever run across United States Marshal Boone?"

"As a matter of fact, I did."

Longarm waited, and when Tyler didn't continue, he grew impatient. "And?"

"Boone ain't the law in Paradise anymore."

"What?"

"You heard me," Tyler said. "He resigned to become the town's mayor. I hear he hand-picked the man who replaced him, and then he bought all the saloons and a couple of the mines. They say that Cletus Boone is rich and that, if you cross him in Paradise, you've signed your own death warrant."

"I see."

Lilly touched his arm. "Custis?"

"What?"

"If Boone isn't a federal lawman anymore, then you

128

don't need to go there and investigate. Do you?"

"Maybe not." Longarm frowned. "Tyler, where is the telegraph office in this town?"

"Just up the street."

"I'd better go there and send a telegram to my boss. Billy Vail will know what I should do at this point, and he can also wire some expense money. I'm broke."

"I've got money enough for all of us to reach California—if you change your mind about being a United States marshal," Lilly said.

"I'll keep your offer in mind, but I still need to contact Billy."

"Well," Lilly snorted, "if I were you, and he said you *still* had to go to Paradise, I'd tell him to go ride a pole."

Longarm had to smile. "You don't understand. Billy is my friend. Besides that, if I don't go to investigate, I can't write off this whole darned trip, and it'll take me months to repay what I've spent."

"Not if you quit your job. San Francisco would seem like heaven with its cool Pacific breezes. That's where we ought to go next."

"I thought you were going back to the ranch."

"Only if you insist on going on to Paradise."

"I've never been a quitter, so I'll finish this job." Longarm turned to the kid. "Why don't you and Miss Lilly find out when the next riverboat that carries passengers is going upriver?"

"Jeb Callaway has a boat for hire," Tyler said. "He'll take us up the river. But he's not to be trusted."

"What does that mean?"

"Well," Tyler said, "it's common knowledge that he will steal your money if you give him half a chance."

"Then we won't give him any chance," Longarm said. "Go find the man and see if you can get him to take us up to where we need to head off to Paradise."

"Yes, sir."

"What am I supposed to do now?" Lilly asked, sounding peevish.

"If I were you, I'd try to scout up some shade and take a rest."

"Shade or no shade, it's still unbearably hot here. I wish I'd never left the ranch."

"With luck, you'll see it again soon," Longarm said, heading up the street. "I'll go and send a telegram and then see what they say about me and ex-marshal Cletus Boone."

Longarm's much anticipated reply from Denver didn't come back until the next morning, and when it did, the message was short but definitely not sweet. It read:

AM SENDING ONE HUNDRED DOLLARS TODAY. **STOP.**
GO TO PARADISE AS DISCUSSED. **STOP.**
MARSHAL CLETUS BOONE IS STILL ON THE FEDERAL
PAYROLL. **STOP.**
ARREST BOONE IF NECESSARY AND TRANSPORT HIM
TO YUMA PRISON. **STOP.**
GOOD LUCK. **STOP.**

"Well," Longarm said to himself as he folded the telegram and placed it in his shirt pocket, "I guess that pretty well lays it out. Just need some money and then a way to reach Paradise."

"Good news?" the telegraph operator asked.

"Not especially," Longarm told him. "I'm Deputy United States Marshal Custis Long, and I'm expecting a hundred dollars to be wired here today."

"As soon as it arrives, I will take it over to the bank. They take care of that business."

"Where's the bank?"

"Just down the street. First National of Yuma."

Longarm glanced up at the clock on the wall. It was only nine in the morning, and the temperature outside was already nudging ninety degrees. "I'll be checking with the bank."

"Do that, Marshal."

Longarm killed an hour looking at horses for sale down at Swenson's Livery before he visited the bank's manager. His travel money hadn't arrived yet, but the man assured him that it probably would by noon. "If you tell me where you're staying," he said, "I'll send a boy to fetch you the moment it arrives from Denver."

"We're hoping to leave town right away."

"So what brings you to our town?"

"I was looking for someone," Longarm replied, purposefully vague.

"Did you find them?"

"I did. Listen, we haven't checked out of the Colorado River Hotel yet, so that's where you should send your boy to let me know when my money arrives from Denver."

"I'll do it. Generally you tip the boy four bits for his trouble."

"Not a problem," Longarm said as he left the bank.

On his way to find Lilly and young Tyler, Longarm considered what Monty's son had told him about Paradise. If Boone had indeed resigned from his office, then that sure didn't square with what Billy had informed him in the telegram. Maybe Boone had just forgotten to tell the government that he had resigned and was collecting a federal paycheck for doing nothing but his own business. If so, the man would be guilty of illegally taking government funds. That alone would be enough of a reason to make an arrest. But Longarm also knew that you didn't just waltz into a rough mining town and clamp the handcuffs on the mayor.

"Might be big trouble ahead," he muttered to himself as he tromped up the street toward the hotel.

Tyler and Lilly were nowhere to be seen when he arrived, so Longarm told the hotel clerk they might be staying another night. "That's good," the sleepy-eyed clerk replied. "We're a little slow in the summer. Not too many visitors this time of year."

"I can see why. Is it this hot all the time?"

"Only from May to October," the clerk told him. "Rest of the year it doesn't get over eighty in the day and the nights are even cooler."

The clerk yawned and became interested in a fly that was buzzing around overhead. Picking up a rolled and tattered newspaper which had obviously been used for this purpose, the man came alive and swore, "If you'll excuse me, I'm going to kill that little son of a bitch!"

"Sure," Longarm said. "Don't let me stand in the way of you having a good time."

It was meant as a humorous remark, but it went right over the man's head as he began to stalk, and then madly swat at, the fly. Before Longarm found a couch upon which to rest in the lobby, the clerk had triumphed and the offending fly had met his terrible end.

The money arrived at two o'clock. Longarm tipped the boy and then collected his funds before going back to the hotel and finding Tyler and Lilly dozing in the hotel lobby.

"Wake up," he told them. "We're heading for Paradise. Tyler, did you talk to Jeb Callaway?"

"Sure did," the kid replied, "but he wants twenty dollars to take us up to the jumping off point."

"That's pretty steep."

"I know, but Jeb was in a saloon, and he was winning at the poker table. Maybe he'll come down on his price if he starts losing all his money."

"Where is this saloon?"

"Down on the waterfront. It's called the River Bar. Want me to come along?"

"Sure," Longarm said, glancing at Lilly. "Why don't you go back up to our rooms and take a real nap."

"Because it's even hotter up there than it is down here."

Longarm knew this to be true. "Tyler and I will be back soon," he said. "Hopefully, we can get under way within the next hour."

Lilly mopped her brow. She was flushed and out of sorts. "I might be dead of this heat before then."

"I doubt that," Longarm told her.

"Well, I'm not going to Paradise!"

"That's your choice."

"Tyler," she asked, turning to the kid, "isn't there some kind of respectable passenger boat that goes far enough up the Colorado River to where I can catch a train back to Mountain City?"

"Yes, ma'am. There's a mail packet with soldiers on board."

Her eyes brightened. "When and where?"

"I'm afraid that it only steams through Yuma once a month, and it just left two weeks ago."

Lilly's closed her eyes and groaned. "I doubt I could survive this town for two more weeks."

"So what are you going to do?" Longarm asked. "Go with us to Paradise . . . or stay here and wait for the mail packet?"

"I guess I'll go with you."

"Could be rough," Longarm warned.

"Of course it could," Lilly snapped. "But I doubt it could be any worse than what we've already been through."

"I hope that's true," Longarm said as he started back outside with Tyler close on his heels. "But there are no guarantees. I'll pay Callaway and see if we can leave at once."

It didn't take long to find the River Bar, and when Longarm stepped inside, he was assaulted with the stench of vomit, urine and cheap Mexican tobacco. The interior of the place was dimly lit, hot and humid, with a motley a collection of riverboat men, prostitutes, down-on-their-luck gamblers, Indians and soldiers. Everyone turned and stared with sullen or even hostile expressions.

Longarm leaned toward Tyler and whispered, "Not a

word about me being a United States marshal. Understand?"

"I sure do." Tyler shifted uneasily on his feet. "I think it would be a good idea to wait outside until Jeb quits playing cards."

"Which one is he?"

"He's the big fella at the far table. The one with the knife scar on his cheek and the red bandanna tied around his neck."

"All right. Maybe you ought to wait outside until me and Callaway have finished our business."

"Not a chance," Tyler said. "Jeb always gets prickly when he's been drinking. As far as I know, he's never been whipped."

"I came to *hire* the man, not fight him."

"You might have to do both," Tyler said. "The truth is, I wouldn't miss what's going to happen next for anything!"

Longarm took a deep breath and waded through dirty sawdust. No one looked up from the card game when he came to a stop, so he said, "Mr. Callaway, my name is Custis Long, and I understand Tyler spoke to you about taking us upriver."

Callaway didn't act as if he'd heard Longarm. He just kept on playing cards. One of the other men at the poker table glanced up at Longarm and grunted, "If I was you, stranger, I'd find something else to do right now."

"Yeah, but you're not me," Longarm snapped. This time, when he spoke to the riverboat man, there was an edge in his voice. "Callaway, we'd like to leave within the hour."

The big man tossed down a shot of whiskey and pitched a three of diamonds and a five of spades into the pile. "Give me two more cards," he growled.

Longarm heard several men at the bar chuckle, but he waited until the hand was played out. Callaway ran a bluff and won a nice pot that Longarm guessed amounted to nearly ten dollars. The other four players were starting to give Longarm dirty looks.

"Callaway," Longarm said, "either get out of that chair and get your boat ready to take us up the river, or we'll find someone else to do the job."

Finally, the big man acknowledged Longarm's presence. Cocking his head sideways, he stared up, revealing a prominent knife scar that began at his throat and went up to his eyebrow, twisting his left eye. The effect gave the big man an evil expression.

"Mister," Callaway said in a deep voice, "you'd be smart to wait until I've had my run at this table, and then maybe we'll talk business. I ain't gonna be bothered by you no more. Understand?"

Longarm's fist shot out to scoop up the deck of cards, then he tossed them to the floor. "Sorry," he said in a quiet voice that mocked the apology, "but I'm not of a mind to wait."

Jeb Callaway shoved his chair back and spun around to face Longarm. "Pick up the cards," he ordered. "Get down on your damned knees and pick 'em up right now!"

"Nope."

Callaway grinned even as his massive fist came up fast and hard. Longarm stepped back and dodged the uppercut a split second before he drove a straight right into the riverboat man's ugly face. Callaway crashed over the poker table, sending men and money flying.

"Why don't we quit right now?" Longarm asked. "Before someone gets hurt."

Callaway let loose with a mighty roar and tackled Longarm. They were equally matched in size and strength, and Callaway landed on top. He slammed his dirty fist down like a hammer, but Longarm was able to twist his head enough so that he received only a glancing blow to his jaw. Even so, he knew that he had better get back on his feet in a hurry, or risk having his face rearranged.

With the bar crowd cheering Jeb Callaway on, Longarm grabbed a broken chair and jammed it upward into Callaway's throat. Then, he bucked the man off and smashed him in the side of his jaw. Callaway's knees buckled and he tossed sawdust into Longarm's face, momentarily blinding him.

Longarm took three tremendous punches that sent him reeling backward before he was able to clear his vision. A huge overhand right would have knocked him silly if he hadn't dodged the blow and driven his shoulder into Callaway's belly and propelled the man into the bar. Glasses and bottles crashed, and men bellowed obscenities as Longarm punished Callaway with a left and a right combination.

Callaway shook his head and wiped blood from his face, then he grabbed a bottle of whiskey. Not bothering to open it, he smashed the neck of the bottle against the bar then poured some of its contents down his throat, eyeing Longarm with grudging respect and a crimson smile.

"You hit hard," he said, dousing his face with the liquor and then pouring more down his gullet. "And you know how to fight. But I'll whip you yet!"

"Talk is cheap. Say, Jeb, why don't we make this fight count?"

"What do you mean?" Callaway asked suspiciously.

"If I whip you, then you take three of us up the river for free."

"And after I whip you?" Callaway demanded, shifting his grip on the broken bottle.

"If you whip me, then I'll pay you a hundred dollars in cash."

"Done!" the man shouted as he came at Longarm, aiming the shattered bottle at his eyes.

Longarm could have drawn his gun and shot the man, but instead he ducked sideways and kicked out at Callaway's knee. The riverboat man screamed as his knee was suddenly bent inward. The big man staggered. Before he could recover, Longarm slammed a brutal punch into his kidney and dropped him in the sawdust.

Callaway was still not quite finished, and he reached into his boot top for a long bowie knife.

"Look out!" Tyler cried in warning. "He'll rip you open!"

Longarm picked up the broken bottle of whiskey and threw it at Callaway's face. The bottle struck the man between the eyes and knocked him sprawling. Longarm landed on Callaway's chest with bent knees knocking the wind out of the man's lungs. Then, he grabbed Callaway's shirt front and hit him twice, the first blow breaking his nose and the second one spreading the blood and cartilage around on his face.

"You're going to kill him!" the bartender shouted, dragging up a shotgun and pointing it at Longarm.

Custis lowered his bloody fists, then stood over the man barely conscious man. "We'll meet you at your steam wheeler in one hour. If you're not there, then we'll take the boat upriver ourselves and beach it at the jump off to Paradise."

Callaway managed to nod his head and then spit blood from his mouth. "I'll be there."

"I expect you will be, or I'll come back here and finish what I started," Longarm told the man as he reached down and helped him to his feet and then to a chair.

Callaway gripped the arms of the chair and shook his head as if to clear a fog from his find.

"One hour," Longarm repeated as he backed away from the man and surveyed the crowd.

Tyler eased up next to Longarm and said, "Jeb will have to kill you now."

"No doubt he'll want to," Longarm said, "but I expect he might just be smart enough to know I'd be able to kill him first."

Longarm said that loud enough for Jeb Callaway to hear and remember the warning. Then, he turned and left the River Bar and went outside.

"Holy cow!" Tyler yelped. "If I hadn't seen it with my

own eyes, I'd never have believed how bad you whipped Jeb!"

"He was half drunk," Longarm explained. "If he hadn't been, it would have been a sight tougher."

"Folks around here will be talking about that fight for years!"

"Let them," Longarm said, his own legs feeling a bit unsteady. He studied the blood on his hands and shirt. "Let's go down to the river, so I can get cleaned up before we go back to the hotel for Lilly."

"You feeling all right?"

"I've felt better."

Tyler was excited and he wanted to talk. "Did you ever fight my pa?"

"Of course not. He was my friend."

"Could he fight like you?"

Longarm's face was numb from the punishment it had taken, but he did manage a crooked smile. "Yeah," he answered, "your father was one hell of a fighter."

"Could he have whipped you?"

"Sure. He could have beat me easy."

"Holy cow!"

Longarm laid his hand across Tyler's shoulder, hoping the kid didn't see how wobbly he was moving. Then, they made their way down to the docks and the water. On their way, neither of them noticed the crowd that had filed out of the River Bar to stare at the big stranger with unconcealed admiration.

Chapter 15

Mindful of having been caught off guard earlier by a riverboat man, Longarm watched Jeb Callaway like a hawk, never for a moment letting down his guard. It was hard getting back on the river and again passing by the landmarks, snags and sand bars that they'd already navigated. But even though Callaway was battered almost beyond recognition, thanks to Longarm's fists, the man was a expert captain and his paddle wheeler, stoked by an immense boiler, pushed them upriver at a remarkable rate of speed.

"All right," the surly captain announced as they approached a familiar but empty landing. "That's where you start for Paradise. Just beyond that rise is a trading post."

"Is there a regular stage line that will take us to Paradise?" Longarm asked.

"No. Since you have no horses, you'll have wait for a supply or maybe an ore wagon to come along. The road to Paradise is hard and dangerous because of Indian attacks. Guess I don't have to tell you I'd shed no tears if you all got scalped."

Lilly shook her head and her expression was bleak. "I can't believe that I ever left Mountain City. And, if I get back there alive, I'll never leave the ranch again."

"Tell you what," Callaway said, "if you don't fancy getting off here, you can stick with me. I may not look like much right now, but I know how to pleasure a woman."

"I'll bet," Lilly said caustically. "But to be honest, I'd rather take my chances with the Indians."

The big captain spat a wad of tobacco juice into the river and turned away. He gave orders for his paddle wheeler to hold just off shore, then turned to Longarm and said, "The three of you get off my boat and do it now."

Fortunately, the bow was low to the water, so it would be easy to disembark. Longarm held one of Lilly's arms, and Tyler took the other as they prepared to help the distressed woman wade to shore. But just as they were going over the side, Tyler twisted around and yelled, "Custis, look out!"

Longarm whirled, hand going for his pistol just as Callaway flung his deadly bowie knife. The captain's aim was off, and the knife whistled past Longarm into the river. Enraged by his failure, Callaway grabbed a pole and swung it at Longarm's head. Ducking under the deadly blow, Longarm fired twice, the shots so closely spaced that they sounded like a single retort.

Callaway staggered, then cupped the fountain of blood that began to spurt from his belly. Staring down at his hands, he shook his head as if in disbelief, then he turned his gaze on Longarm.

"Damn you," he grated before he pitched over the side of his paddle wheeler and landed face down in the shallows. The water turned red around his torso and the current gently pushed him to shore.

Longarm turned his gun on the crew. "Anyone else interested in a fight?"

They backed away until Longarm helped a very pale and frightened Lilly to shore and then up a steep incline to a freighting road. Longarm paused for a moment to shout, "Get your captain out of the river and bury him!"

But the crew acted as if they were glad to finally be rid of their vicious taskmaster. Orders were given and the paddles reversed direction as the vessel backed out into the channel, then turned around in the middle of the Colorado. In less than five minutes, all that was visible of Callaway's boat was a trail of wispy wood smoke rising in the hot, desert air.

"I guess we'd better bury Callaway ourselves," Tyler said, studying Longarm.

The sun was blazing hot, and Longarm knew they had to get to shade. "All right," he conceded, "we'll plant him in the mud."

"But Marshal," Tyler protested, "if we don't drag him up to higher ground and bury him, that body will rise up in the mud when the river floods next spring."

Longarm shielded his eyes from the burning sun. "It doesn't matter anymore," he decided aloud. "The man was no good, and we need to save our strength."

"Tyler is right," Lilly said after long reflection. "It's not right to bury the man in the mud knowing his body will surface. We should give him a fit burial."

"This ground is rocky," Longarm argued. "It would take hours to dig a grave and we don't have a pick or a shovel. We can't scoop the rocks out with our hands."

The three of them stood on the higher ground staring down at Jeb Callaway's body. Finally, Longarm started back down to the river saying, "We'll bury him in the dry sand."

Neither Tyler nor Lilly objected, so Longarm dragged the heavy body out of the water and onto a sandbar. Sagging to his knees, he began to scoop the soft sand up with his bare hands. Lilly and Tyler joined him, and they finished the job within an hour.

"I ought to say a few words over him," Tyler said as they started to walk away.

"Make it quick," Longarm told the young man.

"I will," Tyler replied.

As they began to walk up what was obviously a well-traveled freighting road, Lilly glanced at Custis and said, "Tyler is a fine young man. Despite all he's been through in his young life, at least he still has a good heart."

"Meaning I don't?"

"I didn't say that."

"You didn't need to," Longarm replied. "You think I'm heartless."

"No," Lilly corrected, "I just believe you've seen far too much bloodshed. I knew a surgeon who had worked the battlefields at Shiloh and Bull Run during the war. He said that if a human being saw too much death and mayhem, they either had to get hardened to it . . . or they'd go crazy. Were you a soldier in the war before you became a federal marshal?"

Longarm wasn't in a mood to talk. *Where is that trading post, anyway?* "Lilly," he said, "why don't we just drop this subject?"

"I'll bet you were in the war between the states. I'll bet you've seen more death than I can imagine."

"Enough," Longarm snapped.

"You ought to turn in your badge before you lose whatever humanity you have left."

Longarm licked his cracked lips. "'I'll give you this much . . . you are a very persistent woman."

"And you, Marshal Long, are a very stubborn man."

"If I weren't, I'd have been dead a long time ago," Longarm said, turning to wait for Tyler Kilpatrick to catch up with them.

The grizzled old man who owned the trading post wore pants cut off at the knees and native sandals of woven yucca fibers. He had a long, gray beard that was well stained with tobacco juice which constantly dribbled from both corners of his mouth. He wore what must have once been considered a hat, but was now just a patch of dirty, misshapen felt and his shirt was sleeveless and missing most of its buttons. Despite his age, he had muscular arms and the calves of his legs were deeply tanned, thick and covered with hair as white and thick as frost.

He was a bit hard of hearing, and Longarm had to talk very loud in order to be heard when he told the trader that they needed to reach Paradise.

"You planning on mining there?"

"We have business in Paradise," Longarm said. "How soon can we expect a ride?"

"As a matter of fact," the man said, "you timed it pretty well. I'm expecting a supply wagon in later today. They'll be heading back to Paradise first thing tomorrow morning."

"Good."

The trader sized his new guests up and said, "Since you can't leave until tomorrow, you'll have to spend the night here or in the bush."

"I'm not sleeping out another night," Lilly vowed. "We'll sleep right here where it's safe."

"Wise decision," the trader said, looking extremely pleased. "And fortunately for you folks, I just happen to have some empty cots which I rent at four bits a night."

"Where are they?" Lilly asked.

"In my tent out back."

"Are your mattresses clean?"

"Nothing is clean in these parts, ma'am. And anyway, them cots don't have mattresses. You sleep on blankets. I can sell you new ones . . . if you're persnickety."

"How much?"

"Four dollars each, and they ain't never been used."

"We'll take three," Lilly told the old man.

"Good decision, young lady. The ones on the cots are alive with fleas and lice. And by the way, my name is Otis Gill. Been here for twenty-seven years and used up

143

four Indian wives. Got a good one now, though, and she's a real hard worker."

"What do you have to eat?"

Gill clapped his thick hands together. "As a matter of fact, just yesterday I had my wife butcher a pig. She cut his throat and bled him out real good, then hauled him into a tub out back where he's been boilin' since last evening."

"I thought I could smell something, but I thought it was a dead dog or maybe a rotting cow," Tyler told the man.

"Naw!" Gill replied. "That's just boiling pork. That pig is gonna be real tasty. My wife knows how to season 'em so you'd think the pig was fed nothin' but corn."

Longarm rubbed his empty belly, hoping that the meat tasted better than it was smelling. "I'm sold," he said. "How soon can we eat?"

"Be ready in just a jiffy," Gill promised. "That pig is sure gonna be tasty. Meal will cost you only two bits each, and you can eat all you can hold down in your stomach."

"Sounds good."

"Then follow me into the dining room," the trader told them, as he led the way through his post which, given its location, was surprisingly well stocked with supplies that ran from ropes, to paddles, blankets, beaver traps and a sizable collection of old and rusting percussion rifles that Longarm would not have attempted to shoot for any amount of money.

Longarm glanced up at the ceiling and saw that half the roof was missing. "What happened?"

Gill craned his neck. "Wind blew part of it away about five years ago. Haven't quite got around to having my wife fix it yet."

"Don't you worry about all your trading goods getting wet?"

"Naw! You see, it don't hardly ever rain. Maybe an inch or two a year. When it does, I just move stuff around and put the rest under a canvas tarp."

Longarm nodded with understanding, and they passed into a room about twenty square feet with several rough tables and benches.

"You can sit here and rest," Gill told them. "If you want some whiskey or tobacco, I got the best."

"I'll have some of both," Longarm told the cheerful man.

Gill smiled. "They ain't cheap. Everything I got has to be floated up the Colorado all the way from Yuma. And to get to Yuma, it has to come clear around the Baja from San Diego or Frisco."

"I've got cash," Longarm said, mopping his brow and settling down on a bench. "Bring the whiskey."

"Sure will," Gill answered with a wink.

The pig that Gill's wife had butchered, boiled and seasoned had tasted surprisingly good, but its effects were devastating. Longarm, Lilly and Tyler spent most of the night running out into the bushes, and it wasn't a pretty sight.

"I feel half poisoned," Lilly whispered weakly the next morning as she lay on her cot between her two companions. "We should never have eaten that pork."

"I'm not sure that it was pork," Tyler moaned. "I still think he boiled us a dead dog. Or maybe a coyote."

Longarm was trying to fight down another attack of the runs, and it was a touch-and-go, moment-to-moment situation. "I'm gonna have a few words with Otis when I feel I can stand still for more than a minute. I swear his wife almost killed us!"

"And she seemed so nice," Lilly said, her voice reflecting amazement. "And did you notice how much she and her husband ate?"

"Yeah," Longarm said. "Almost as much as I did. I wonder if they're able to get off *their* backs this morning."

Just then, the old trader stuck his head into the tent and grinned. "Mornin' folks! Ready for some breakfast?"

"Get out of here!" Longarm bellowed, the effort giving his bowels a fresh incentive to riot.

Gill looked hurt until Longarm shot past him holding his gut and heading out into the bushes. "Ma'am, has your man got the Mexican quick step this morning?"

"We all do," Lilly said, unable to keep anger out of her voice. "What was that we ate last night?"

"Why, fresh killed pork!" Gill frowned. "You know that. 'Member how we all found some hog bristles in the meat and used 'em to pick our teeth after we ate?"

Lilly sighed. "Yes. Come to think of it, I do remember."

"How about some coffee laced with whiskey? It'll settle your guts down and make you all feel a lot better."

"No, thanks. I think I'll just lie here and die quietly."

The trader shook his head. "Well, I'll tell my wife that you three aren't quite ready for breakfast and to hold off on the fried lizard."

"That's what you were going to fix us?"

"Well," Gill admitted, "it ain't all lizard. There's some rattler and horned toad meat in there too . . . but it's all seasoned real nice."

"Ahhh!" Lilly groaned. "Go away!"

Gill shrugged and disappeared. A few moments later, Longarm reappeared, buttoning his pants and still holding his belly. He flopped down on his cot and rolled his head to face Lilly. "What did Gill have to say about the food?"

"He wanted to know if we wanted breakfast."

"Might be settlin' on our poor bellies."

"No, it wouldn't," Lilly said. "Trust me that it wouldn't."

"But . . ."

Just then Tyler jumped up and headed out of the tent on the run. They could hear him retching and having a bad time out in the bushes. Longarm shook his head.

"Maybe what we need is a little coffee braced with the hair of the dog," he said.

146

"Don't talk to me," Lilly told him as she closed her eyes.

Longarm could see that the woman wasn't going to try to make the best of the situation, so he closed his own eyes and went back to sleep.

Chapter 16

Their ride to Paradise was long, hot and bumpy. The road was little more than a dirt track filled with potholes, and by the time that they reached the remote mining town, Longarm, Lilly and Tyler felt as if they had been beaten.

They paid the driver and stood at the edge of town feeling drained and weak from travel and food poisoning. Longarm slowly surveyed the town's main street buildings and then studied the hills pocked with mine tailings. He could see several hundred miners working their individual claims, and he marveled at how much men would endure to find wealth in such unforgiving and inhospitable surroundings.

"Tyler, where do all these people get their water?"

"There's a spring about five miles to the east of town. They're constantly hauling in water. Cletus Boone owns most of that business as well as about everything else in Paradise."

"I don't see his copper mines."

"They're also east of town." Tyler shaded his eyes and pointed to a small hole in the hillside and its accompanying mound of reddish earth. "That's where I staked my own claim. Worked it for a month and ran out of money. Had to go back to the river and earn some more, and then I was coming back here to strike it rich."

"You're pretty young to have already been infected with gold fever," Lilly said. "You'll do far better up in Mountain City."

"I don't know about that," the kid told her. "You say my father left me a cabin and some land, but that won't put beans on the table. I'll still have to find some way to make a living."

"There are plenty of things you can do where I come from."

"Such as?"

"On the Rocking J, we're always looking for young, willing men to learn to be cowboys."

"I might like that, all right."

"I expect you would," Lilly told him.

"But I sure would have liked to have struck it rich up there on my claim. I still feel that if I could have hung on for six months, I'd have surely discovered gold or silver."

Longarm had his doubts. "Like all those other men still killing themselves up on those hillsides? Trust me, Tyler. Mining is a hard, dangerous occupation, and only one in ten thousand ever wind up with anything more than a bad back and empty pockets."

The kid nodded, but still didn't look fully convinced that he couldn't have hit pay dirt.

"And I'll tell you something else," Longarm added as they started up the street toward the Coachman Hotel. "Even if you had been lucky enough to have struck it rich, you'd still have had to have figured out a way to stay alive and keep your new found wealth. Why, in this kind of a lawless town, everyone would have been trying to either kill you . . . or steal you blind."

"I expect that's true. I saw more than one miner who had a few ounces of gold in his pouch wind up with his throat cut from ear to ear. Or shot in the back."

Tyler glanced at the sky, eyes troubled. "I remember that there were plenty of times when miners just disappeared, and maybe a day or two later, you'd see a flock of vultures circling lower and lower in the sky. It wasn't hard to figure what those birds were getting ready to feed upon."

Longarm nodded with understanding, then said, "We'll get rooms at the Coachman and rest up for a day or two before I confront Mayor Boone."

"Why the delay?" Lilly asked.

"Because I'm in no shape to take the man on if he chooses to be difficult."

"Oh," Tyler said, "Mr. Boone will turn out to be a lot more than difficult. My bet is that once he finds out you're a lawman come to arrest him, he'll set about figuring the easiest way to have you killed."

They passed a tent saloon, and Longarm was very aware that he and his companions were attracting a good deal of attention. Lilly was aware of it, too, because she said, "Why is everyone staring at us?"

"Because we're out of the ordinary," Longarm replied. "But even more than that, because you're a pretty woman."

Lilly scoffed, and her hand flew to her sunburned and wind-chafed face, then to her dirty, disheveled hair. "Pretty? Why that almost makes me laugh. I look terrible."

"You're still pretty to these men," Tyler assured her. "They don't see many white women. And those that do come to Paradise sure aren't what anyone would call 'lookers.'"

"For a boy of thirteen, you are far too worldly," she told him.

Tyler just shrugged his broad but bony shoulders and replied matter-of-factly, "A kid grows up fast and hard in this country . . . or else he dies. I figured that out right away."

Lilly tried to give Tyler a hug, to let him know that she understood, but he pulled away and said, "Here's the hotel. You'd better have money to give 'em right now or we'll sleep outdoors."

151

"Lilly has plenty of money," Longarm said. "Isn't that right?"

"I suppose," she told him, as she rummaged in her bag and handed Longarm a roll of bills, then added, "But I want back my change."

"I figured as much."

There were only about a dozen wooden buildings in Paradise, and the Coachman Hotel was the most impressive, with a second story that towered over everything else in the rough, desert mining town.

Longarm got them a pair of adjoining rooms and ordered baths and meals for two days.

"Where you from?" the hotel clerk asked when Longarm left that part of the register entry blank.

"Hell," Lilly snapped.

Straight-faced, the clerk said, "I find that impossible to believe."

"Why?"

"Because *this* is hell."

"Then why do you stay?" Lilly asked.

"Same reason everyone else does . . . money."

"But you're a hotel clerk."

"That's right, but since everyone here has gold fever, they have to pay me three times what I'd make in Yuma or Tucson. So while the miners work like dogs in the hot sun, I have it easy, and I get a free room and meals to boot. I'm saving more money than I've ever saved in my life, and I plan to leave here when the ore plays out with enough saved to buy a nice house and retire for the rest of my days."

"Now that makes sense," Lilly told him as the man handed them keys to their rooms and then pointed to a stairway that would lead up to the second floor.

When they reached the second-floor landing, the heat was almost unbearable. "Why, it must be a hundred and fifty degrees up here!" Lilly cried.

"Closer," Longarm added, "to a hundred and ten."

He unlocked the doors to their rooms and strode over

to a window, throwing it opening in the faint hope of catching a cooling breeze. "This will have to do us," he said. "We'll bathe, rest easy for a day and eat some good food. We'll all feel a lot better by this time tomorrow."

Tyler went off to rest in the adjoining room and closed the door connecting their rooms. Lilly sank down on the bed and looked around at the bare walls and dirty hardwood floor. "I won't be able to stand it here for more than a couple of nights. I'm worn down, and I've got to get out of this hot country before I die."

"I hope to wrap up my business soon."

"Oh?" she asked, raising her eyebrows with obvious skepticism. "And exactly how to do you propose to do that?"

"I'm not sure. But I'll figure out something."

"Sure. Tomorrow you'll clean up and go visit Mayor Cletus Boone, and after shaking his hand and introducing yourself as a federal marshal, you'll calmly tell him that he is under arrest and that you intend to take him to the Yuma Prison."

"It probably won't go that smooth," Longarm said, beginning to feel irritated by her sarcasm.

"I'm sure that it won't! What I think will happen is that by this time tomorrow, Tyler and I will be shopping for someone to build your casket and plant you in the ground real quick, so we can get out of this awful town alive."

Longarm kicked off his boots and stretched out on the bed. "That's what I most admire about you, Lilly."

"What's that?"

"Your sense of humor."

She kicked off her own shoes, then removed her clothes and sank down on the bed beside him. "I'm sorry to be so depressing, Custis. But for the life of me, I can't see how you're going to arrest the mayor without getting either killed or tarred and feathered."

"There's always a way," he told her. "But I'll admit that this time especially, I'm going to have to be very smart about it."

"The smart thing to do would be for all of us to go straight back to Yuma and then you telegraph your boss in Denver saying that you'd prefer to go on living. Then, we would return to Mountain City, help Tyler do whatever he wants to do and have long, happy and peaceful lives."

Longarm managed to dredge up a weary grin. "That does sound pretty good at the moment."

"Of course it does!" Lilly turned to face Longarm. "I've never felt so discouraged as I do right now. I have this feeling that we're walking into far more than we can possibly imagine ... and all of it is bad."

Longarm pulled her close. "Let's get a bath, a couple good meals in our empty bellies and a fair night's sleep. Come tomorrow, things are just bound to look more promising."

"I don't believe that," she told him, "but it sounds good."

Longarm fell asleep, and he didn't wake up until someone pounded on their door shouting that their bath water was ready.

They slept well that night, and it was amazing what good food, a bath and a solid night's rest could do to rejuvenate a badly punished body. Longarm felt like a completely new man when he checked his sidearm and brushed the dust from his Stetson.

"We'll be here," Tyler said, looking worried. "You sure that you don't want me to come along? I can use a gun."

"No," Longarm told the kid, "I would prefer to do this myself. Is there a jail in this town?"

"They use a little rock house for the really bad prisoners," Tyler told him. "But mostly, in Paradise they either kill or run off troublemakers."

"Do you know if there is a judge in these parts?"

"There isn't one. Mr. Boone is the justice of the peace and he sometimes holds court. The last time I was here, his jury sentenced two men to hang, but since they were real big and everyone was afraid that their weight would break the livery barn's rafters, they decided to shoot the prisoners instead."

Longarm could hardly believe what he'd just heard. "They put 'em in front of a firing squad?"

"That's right," Tyler replied. "But everyone chosen to shoot the guilty was dead drunk, and they sure made a mess of those two fellas."

"What crime did the pair commit to earn the right to get riddled by a drunken mob?"

"They stole a pair of Mayor Boone's best horses and ran them nearly to death trying to reach Tucson with money they'd robbed."

"I see."

"It's said in these parts that when Cletus Boone became the judge in Paradise, justice became swift and unmerciful."

"There is no justice here," Longarm told the kid a moment before he left their hotel room. "There's just Cletus Boone playing God . . . only he *isn't* God, and he's about to find that out. Where can I find the man?"

"He has a mansion at the far end of town, but he usually hangs out at Boone's Saloon."

"Thanks," Longarm said. He closed the door knowing that Lilly and Tyler considered him a walking dead man, but he'd faced long odds before and won. Maybe . . . somehow . . . his luck would hold in Paradise.

Chapter 17

It was not hard to find the saloon, and when Longarm stepped inside, he was surprised at both its size and opulence. There were fine paintings on every wall, with gilded and ornately carved frames that hinted at European craftsmanship, heavy crystal chandeliers, painted wooden floors and a polished mahogany bar at least forty feet long. Behind the bar, two men dressed in starched white shirts and black ties waited to serve the customers.

Given that it was only mid-morning, the saloon was quite busy. Longarm saw card games being played at four different tables, and there were at least a dozen men at the bar, most of them miners or merchants.

"Howdy," one of the bartenders said in greeting when Longarm approached. He was about six feet tall, middle-aged and going to fat, but his scarred knuckles and broken nose told Longarm that he had once been a professional fighter. "What's your pleasure this morning?" he asked, rolling his still thickly muscled shoulders.

"I'm looking for Mayor Cletus Boone."

"What for?" the bartender asked with feigned indifference.

"I've got a proposition for him."

"A *business* matter?"

"You could call it that." Longarm twisted around and surveyed the setting. "Nice place."

"It's the finest saloon between Tucson and San Diego. See this bar?" The man patted it like he would his pet dog.

"Yep."

"Came all the way from Spain! Finest wood you can find anywhere in the world."

"It's handsome, all right," Longarm agreed. "I didn't expect to see something like this in a town this size."

"Well," the man said, shining glasses and giving Longarm a broad smile, "you aren't the first newcomer to say that, and I doubt that you'll be the last."

"The mines in this area must really be producing."

"They are! Hardly a week goes by that we don't have a new strike or discover a fresh vein of pay dirt in one of the existing mines."

"That's good to hear," Longarm told the bartender. "So how about pointing Mr. Boone out to me, so we can discuss business."

"That's him over there in the booth with that lady. But he doesn't like to be approached without me coming over first to state the nature of your business. You see, Mr. Boone is a very busy and important man. In case you didn't know it, he owns most of the town and is richer than a king."

"Well," Longarm said, "he doesn't look very busy right now, so I expect I can introduce myself."

"No, you can't."

Longarm caught the tone of warning, and the bartender's smile had frozen on his scarred but still rugged face. "What did you say?"

"It would be breaking the rules if you just went over there and interrupted Mr. Boone. So why don't you give me your name and state your business, so I can find out if my boss is willing to take the time to see you, now?"

"What the hell," Longarm said, as if the matter really wasn't very important. "All right. My name is Custis

Long, and I'm here to discuss . . . a matter of the law."

"The law? I thought you said you wanted to talk to him about business?"

"Well, the law is my business. Just tell Mr. Boone that I'm very curious to know if he still considers himself to be a federal marshal."

"Are you a lawman?"

"I think that I've done enough explaining," Longarm told the bartender. "Just go do as I say."

The bartender did not like taking orders, and he leaned across the bar and said, "I think you ought to leave this saloon."

"Not a chance." Longarm didn't want to play word games anymore. Better to just turn his cards face up on the table and let the chips fall where they may. Having made that decision, he started across the floor toward the only booth in the saloon.

The bartender was fast and silent on his feet, but he accidentally bumped a chair as he overtook Longarm. With only a moment's warning, Longarm ducked sideways and managed to avoid the blow aimed for the base of his neck. Spinning around, he shot an uppercut to the bartender's soft belly. The punch traveled less than a foot, but it had an immediate and dramatic effect. The bartender's cheeks blew out and his mouth flew open. Longarm shoved him over an empty table.

All eyes swivelled to Longarm as he walked up to the booth and said in a voice loud enough for everyone to hear, "Hello, Cletus. I'm Deputy United States Marshal Custis Long from Denver."

At that moment, had a mouse squeaked, it would have sounded louder than a passing freight train.

Former Marshal Boone was so surprised by Longarm's announcement that his jaw dropped. He was thick rather than tall and in his early thirties, with an aquiline nose and square jaw. His hair was sandy as were his eyebrows and he still had a dash of freckles across his cheeks. All together, Boone portrayed a youth and innocence that was totally disarming until you met his eyes and saw that they were as blue, hard and brittle as turquoise.

The woman sitting next to Boone was stunning. Her hair was black and she had the mysterious and mesmerizing beauty of a gypsy woman, the kind that told men's fortunes in the big Eastern cities and then robbed them of their senses and money. Longarm had trouble keeping his eyes off the woman as she studied him in return, her full lips offering only the barest hint of a smile.

"So," Boone said, quickly recovering from his surprise. "You are the famous Longarm. I've heard about you for years, but never expected we'd finally meet."

"Now that we have, why don't you introduce me to your beautiful friend?"

"Of course! Forgive me my lapse of good manners. Aurora, this is Deputy Marshal Custis Long, a legend among federal law officers of the West."

Longarm was about to tip his hat but he heard the fallen bartender behind him groan and then utter a vile curse. He turned and saw the man reaching for a weapon inside his vest, no doubt either a derringer or a knife.

"I wouldn't do that," Longarm warned.

The man's eyes went to those of his boss and, receiving an unspoken message, he crawled away, still heaving and gasping for air.

"Sit down," Boone said with a smile. "And don't take Elam too seriously. He has a tendency to be over-protective."

"I could arrest him for attempted assault."

"I suppose you could," Boone agreed. "But then what? I'm the justice of the peace here and . . . since Elam was acting on my behalf, I'd probably let him off with nothing but a small fine and maybe a few words of warning."

Longarm slid into the booth so that the beautiful Aurora was to his left, giving him the advantage of more space between himself and Boone. "I hope I'm not interrupting something important between you."

"Not at all. We were just passing the time of day. Aurora and I were married only last week."

"Is that right?" Longarm responded. "Congratulations, but I'm afraid you might have to postpone a honeymoon."

Boone raised his eyebrows. "And why would we do that?"

"Because you've been collecting the pay of a federal officer while acting as the mayor of this town."

"Is that a crime?"

"Of course it is," Longarm answered. "I've also been told that you have been extorting money from the other Paradise business owners which, as a federal officer, you know is illegal."

Boone's eyebrows lifted. "Extortion? Now I wonder who would spread such ridiculous rumors?"

"It's a known fact," Longarm said, aware that he was on thin ice, because there was probably no one left in Paradise willing or stupid enough to testify against someone as powerful as the mayor.

"Well," Boone said, "what I think we ought to do is to go over to my office, sit down and have a nice long talk. I'm sure that I can clear up whatever misconceptions you might have gathered about me and my business interests."

"Fine," Longarm said, "but what about Aurora?"

"I don't need a man's constant attention," she told him. "I know how to amuse myself, even in Paradise."

Longarm studied her face for a deeper meaning, but she was inscrutable and that was all the more intriguing. "Perhaps we will meet again later."

"I don't think so, Marshal Long."

"And why is that?"

She shrugged and gave him a sad smile. "It is not fated."

"What a pity."

"Hey!" Boone exclaimed as Longarm and Aurora studied each other intensely. "I've heard of your reputation as a lady's man, so let's go before I get real jealous."

He'd tried to make light of the remark, but Longarm

knew Boone was already jealous. No matter. In fact, it was probably a good idea to keep the man off balance.

"All right," Longarm said, laughter coming to his lips, "let's go and have our talk."

"Excuse us, my dear," Boone said, coming to his feet and then making a big show of kissing his bride. "I'll be back before very long."

Longarm winked at the woman and said, "I'll probably be back as well."

Boone's control slipped, and Longarm didn't miss the sudden hardening of his expression. He was obviously upset as he stomped out of the saloon and into the sunlight. "My office is just up the street."

"Fine saloon you have there, Cletus."

Boone swung around and faced him. "Call me Mayor."

"Oh, sure," Longarm said innocently. "I forgot. But are you still wearing your badge?"

"Hell, no!"

"But you are still taking a federal paycheck."

It wasn't a question, it was a fact, and it caused the man to freeze in his tracks. "Marshal Long," he said, biting off his words, "I'm beginning to wonder if you're going to be a problem."

"I sure hope not," Longarm said, deciding that the best place to make the arrest was in the privacy of Boone's office rather than on the street or in his saloon where so many men owed the mayor their allegiance. "But I'm afraid that we might have some problems to work out."

"Nothing that two intelligent men can't do if they don't lose perspective," Boone said. "Did you really look at my mining town? Because even if you did, you'd never suspect that we're producing nearly ten thousand dollars worth of ore a week."

Longarm whistled softly. "That's quite a haul."

"You bet it is," Boone said, filling his lungs and surveying his domain. "And while I'm not fool enough to think that that production will last forever, I believe that the ore will hold at least another year. By then, I'll be one of the richest men in Arizona, if not the entire West."

"I can believe that."

"Then believe that I won't allow anything to come between me and my plans for the future. When I leave this town, it will be to go on to even bigger and better things."

Longarm was intrigued enough to ask, "Such as?"

"Politics," Boone said forcefully. "I mean to become the mayor of Tucson and then the governor of the territory. When we get statehood, I'll go to Washington as a United States senator. And after that, well," he shrugged, "who can say?"

"You're very ambitious."

"Of course I am," Boone said, starting to walk again. "Why, less than a year ago, I was just another lawman eking out a living and watching other, less talented people prosper."

"But that all changed very suddenly, huh?"

"You bet it did! I recognized that I was in a unique position to become someone special. All I needed to do was to use my talent and ambition not only for self gain, but for the benefit of Paradise."

"So you went into politics."

"Exactly. I replaced the mayor and . . ."

"Whoa! I'm curious," Longarm said, studying the man's expression carefully. "Exactly how did you do that?"

"I ran a strong campaign and was elected by a vast majority of the town's voters. Here's my office," Boone said, using a key to unlock his door. "Come inside. It's a bit early in the day, but I have some French brandy that you'll appreciate. Have you ever been to France?"

"Can't say as I have," Longarm replied, stepping inside the office and finding it just as opulent as expected, with a desk that appeared to have been carved and constructed by the same craftsmen who made the saloon's impressive bar.

"I haven't either," Boone said, "but Aurora has. She's been all over Europe. She comes from a very rich and prominent family in Madrid, Spain. My bride knows many important people . . . not only in Spain . . . but all over Europe."

"Do say."

"That's right. And you might be wondering what brought her to a place like Arizona."

"Yeah," Longarm agreed. "That would have eventually crossed my mind."

"Well," Boone said proudly, "I met her in Tucson. She was staying with some distant relatives that could trace their ancestors back to the Spaniards that first settled in Mexico."

"How about that."

"The moment I laid eyes on that woman, I knew that I had to make her mine. And so I wooed her in the old way that ladies of royal blood expect to be wooed. But her uncle objected, and so we eloped and came back to Paradise."

"You eloped?"

"Yes," Boone told him. "By then, we had fallen madly in love. She is crazy about me, of course. And when I become the mayor of Tucson, her uncle will be so proud that he will fall down and kiss my boots."

"Well," Longarm said, nearly gagging at Boone's colossal self-importance, "then I guess when you become the *governor*, her uncle will probably kiss not only your boots . . . but also your ass."

Again, Boone's jaw dropped and it took him a moment to recover. Finally, he asked in a voice that was barely civil, "Longarm, are you making fun of me?"

"Of course not!"

"Why don't we just get our business over, and then you can leave Paradise and I'll return to Aurora?" Boone said with more than a trace of impatience.

"I'm afraid that won't be possible."

"Why not?"

"Because I have orders from Marshal Billy Vail. You do remember him, don't you?"

"Of course. He's a fat little toad. A government pencil pusher grown soft in his desk chair."

It was Longarm's turn to take offense. "Billy is a good friend of mine. He was out in the field when we were in knickers, and he would fool you in a fight."

"I'm not interested in your friend Billy Vail. You're the one that concerns me."

Longarm had been sitting in a very nice office chair but now he stood and said, "I'm afraid that I have been sent here to arrest you and take you to Yuma."

The man rocked back in his desk chair. "You can't be serious!"

"I'm afraid I am."

"I won't go."

Longarm reached across his waist and drew his Colt .44-.40 and said, "I kind of expected that answer, so I guess we'll just have to do this the hard way."

"Are you mad?"

"No. I'm just an honest, hard working, nobody lawman trying to do my job. If you're innocent of taking a federal paycheck long after resigning to become mayor, and of extorting money and ordering men to be cut down by a drunken-jury-turned-firing-squad, then you'll be set free. But, if not . . ."

"You'll never pull this off," Boone said, placing both hands on his desk, fingers splayed and adorned with heavy gold rings. "I run this town. We won't take fifty steps down the street before you'll have more trouble on your hands than you can imagine."

"If anyone tries to stop me, I'll have to arrest them, too."

Boone actually laughed. "I think the sun has fried your brain!"

"You can think whatever you want, but it doesn't matter. I've come a long, hard way to arrest you, and that's what I'm doing. Now, are you going to come peacefully, or do I have to pistol-whip and carry your body out of this office?"

Boone had risen out of his chair, but now he sat down again. With great effort, he said, "Why don't we use our heads and do the intelligent thing?"

"Which is?"

"I pay you more money than you can make as a lawman in the next five years and you disappear. Leave town while you can still walk and draw a breath."

"And how far would you let me get before you sent a mob to kill me?"

"I'd let you go free," Boone told him. "I'd send you away a far wealthier and happier man. One that could toss his badge in the Colorado River and make a life for himself, instead of groveling from payday to payday with nothing to show for his life except scars and maybe a worthless certificate of appreciation from someone as insignificant as Billy Vail."

"I see."

Boone steepled his fingers, leaned across his desk and whispered, "I'll give you two thousand dollars to go back to Denver and tell them that I am innocent of whatever it is they think I have done wrong."

"And what about the paycheck you've been receiving from the federal government?"

Boone waved his hand as if the matter were of little concern. "My mistake. I'll refund all the money, and you can either run off with it or turn it in to the government. I don't care. We both know that this whole thing is a sham."

"But is it?"

"Of course!" Boone cried. "Don't you understand? I've gotten rich and powerful and your bosses are jealous. This has nothing to do with right or wrong."

"I disagree," Longarm told him. "You've used your federal authority to intimidate, extort and probably to eliminate the opposition. You've no doubt murdered a bunch of people to get to the place of power where you are right now. I can't let that pass. You've abused what I respect most . . . the law of the land."

"Ha! An idealist! A pure-as-the-driven-snow idealist! All right, then, how about *five* thousand dollars in gold?"

In reply, Longarm pointed his gun across the desk at Boone. "You're under arrest. I'll be taking you back to Yuma."

The man fell back in his chair. "I absolutely won't go! Marshal Long, are you going to shoot me? If you do, you're also a dead man. If you don't, there's no sense in any more talk between us. Make up your mind. I've given you my best offer, and now it's your move."

Longarm realized that Boone wasn't bluffing. The man would rather be killed than have his lofty dreams shattered. And since a gunshot would bring half the town down on him, killing Boone would be tantamount to an act of suicide.

"Well?" Boone demanded impatiently, his eyes steely and his voice husky with confidence. "What's it to be, Longarm?"

"You win," Longarm said. "I'll take the five thousand in gold."

A broad, triumphant grin creased his face. "Ha! Now you're showing good sense. But first, I want a letter written in your hand stating that you have found me innocent of all charges."

"What good would that do?" Longarm asked.

"I'd want something to show for my money. Also, I might decide to send it to your superiors."

"All right. Give me a paper and pen."

"I'll dictate exactly what you are to write," Boone ordered.

"Fine."

Longarm was trying to buy a few moments to decide what options he had left. Since walking away from a guilty man wasn't an option, and shooting him to death in his office chair was also out of the question, that meant that the only thing he could do was to render Cletus Boone helpless and then attempt to secrete him out of Paradise. If successful, Lilly and Tyler might be able to reach the river and then even Yuma before a call to arms was heralded.

"I'll get the paper and ink," Boone said, pushing his chair back and reaching into one of the lower drawers of his office desk.

Longarm's hand reached across his waist unseen and then he pulled his gun out and, just as Boone was starting to raise his head and place a sheet of stationery down on his desk, Longarm pistol-whipped the man across the forehead.

Mayor Boone's eyes rolled up in his head and his chin struck his desktop. He was out cold.

Longarm jumped up and pulled Boone out of his chair. Using the man's own shoelaces, he quickly tied his hands behind his back and then bound his ankles. There was a back door to the mayor's office and Longarm rushed over and tore it open.

It was an alley of sorts, filled with outhouses and all kinds of junk and rubbish.

I'll put him in the outhouse, Longarm thought, *and then I'll find Lilly and Tyler. After that, all we need to do is to get ahold of a buckboard and a canvas tarp to cover Boone while we make our escape from Paradise.*

Longarm dragged Boone out of his office and sat him upright in the shitter. It wasn't easy or pleasant work, but it would have to do. The mayor's head lolled against the side of the smelly little structure and Longarm tried his best to lock the door but was unsuccessful.

Now to the hotel to retrieve his friends, and then he'd rent, borrow or steal a buckboard and tarp.

Yes, he thought as he hurried away, *my luck is holding and I think I can pull this off!*

Chapter 18

"I can't believe what you've just done!" Lilly cried. "If we're caught trying to abduct the man who apparently owns this town lock, stock and barrel, why . . . we'll be mobbed and murdered!"

"She's right," Tyler agreed. "At least half of Paradise works for Mr. Boone and they aren't about to let us take him back to Yuma."

But Longarm shook his head. "Don't your understand? There's no doubt in my mind that Cletus Boone used his United States marshal's badge and authority to get a stranglehold on this town. And then he used that position to intimidate and probably murder anyone who opposed him. The townspeople and the miners will probably celebrate when they find out he's been sent to prison."

"What about his wife?" Lilly asked.

"What about her?"

"She's not going to just stand still and let someone rob her of her meal ticket."

Longarm remembered back to the few minutes he'd had to observe and take the measure of Aurora Boone. "I have a feeling," he told his friends, "that Mrs. Aurora Boone wouldn't mind getting control of her husband's holdings."

"What makes you think that?"

"I just have a hunch that she's not quite the aristocratic royalty that Cletus thinks she is. I'm a pretty good judge of character, and I can tell you that Aurora is tough as nails and probably a phony."

Lilly and Tyler exchanged glances, and then the boy said, "I've seen her, and she's beautiful."

"That she is," Longarm agreed. "And no doubt just as ambitious as her husband. No, I'm quite sure that Aurora would not only not try to stop us from ridding Paradise of her husband, but she might even be willing to help."

"You're making a lot of assumptions . . . any one of which could get us killed."

"Maybe so, but we're wasting time talking. I've got to find a buckboard and a fast team of horses. I hit Boone awfully hard, but he might wake up in that outhouse, and then there would be hell to pay."

"Maybe he fell through the hole and suffocated," Tyler said with a grin. "Now wouldn't that be one hell of way to die?"

Longarm could see the humor but said nothing. It was time to find a wagon and get out of Paradise.

Finding a wagon hadn't been that difficult. Actually, they'd just gone to the livery and used Lilly's money to buy one, saying that they were heading off to Tucson and they needed a pair of strong, fast horses and a tarp to cover their supplies. The liveryman hadn't asked any questions because he'd gotten top dollar.

"He charged us twice what this wagon and these horses are worth!" Lilly groused as Longarm drove the buckboard around behind Mayor Boone's office.

"Yeah," Longarm agreed, "But he threw in a hundred pounds of oats and two full, fifty-gallon water barrels, which I expect might come in handy if we need to cut across the desert and head for Tucson."

"And why on earth would we do that?"

"To save our necks if we get overtaken by a vigilante committee."

"There it is," Longarm said, driving the buckboard up to the outhouse. "I sure hope that he didn't wake up and get away."

Longarm reined in the team of bay geldings and jumped down to throw open the little door.

"Oh man," he whispered, staring into the outhouse.

"Is he gone?" Tyler cried.

"No . . . even worse."

Both Tyler and Lilly jumped down and joined Longarm in staring at Mayor Cletus Boone, who sat slumped over sideways with his throat cut from ear to ear. The blood was already congealing, and the place was swarming with black flies. The murder weapon, a large, bone-handled jackknife, was lying between the dead man's feet. Longarm folded the blade and wrapped it in his handkerchief before dropping it into his pocket as evidence.

"Ugggh!" Lilly staggered backward, covering her face and shaking her head.

Tyler just gaped at the dead man until Longarm drew him back and grabbed Boone by the shirt. He dragged the heavy corpse out and then said, "Tyler, let's get him into the buckboard."

"What are we going to do now?"

"I'm not sure yet," Longarm admitted. "But it's not right that he sit in there with the stench and the flies."

They managed to get the mayor into the back of the wagon and then they drove on up the alley, all of them lost in a communion of stunned silence.

"We can't just leave town with their dead mayor and not say anything," Lilly finally said when they were several miles east of Paradise. "Custis, you're the federal law officer. What *can* we do?"

"I intend to find out who murdered him."

"You mean, go back to Paradise?"

"How else could I find out?"

"But . . ."

"I'm thinking," Longarm answered with a hint of exasperation. His mind was racing as he tried to think of some way to handle this unusual situation without putting Tyler or Lilly's life in jeopardy. "Just give me a few minutes of quiet."

Lilly clamped her jaw shut tight and shook her head. "I swear that if I ever get back to Mountain City, I'll never leave the Rocking J again."

Tyler dipped his chin in agreement. "I'm never coming back either, providing we don't get lynched."

"That isn't going to happen," Longarm told them as they finally got into open country and beyond the mining town and its activity.

"I'd like to know why not," Lilly said.

"Because . . . because I figure there's only one person knows who murdered Mayor Boone, and that's the one that did it."

"So?"

"The one that did it might well be the one that had the most to gain by his death."

Lilly shook her head. "But you said that most everyone in Paradise would stand to gain by the mayor's death."

"That's right, but I'd like to know who stood to gain from it the most."

"Any idea who that would be?"

"As a matter of fact, I do have an idea."

"Who?"

"His beautiful bride."

Lilly's eyes widened with surprise. "Do you actually believe that a woman could have done such a terrible thing?"

"Why not? Boone was knocked out cold. Whoever did it couldn't risk using a gun, because the shot would have attracted attention. So they stabbed Cletus to death. Makes sense to me that a woman could have done it as easily as a man."

"You're really grasping at straws," Lilly told him.

"That's true. But I'm going to Paradise and pretend as if nothing happened. It won't take long before the town realizes that its mayor is missing. And when that happens, maybe I'll be able to figure out who *isn't* surprised, and you can bet that I'll be watching Aurora Boone."

"And while you're doing that, what are we supposed to do? Drive into the desert and bury the body?"

"No," Longarm said. He raised his arm and pointed to the east. "Can you see that mine tailing about a quarter mile up that little dirt road that climbs into the hills?"

"Yes."

"Where there's a tailing there is a mine. Isn't that right, Tyler?"

"I guess," the kid said, still not getting Longarm's drift. "But . . ."

"We'll bury Cletus Boone in the mine and cover him up. If we have to exhume the body later, that won't be difficult."

"I'm not digging up any dead bodies!" Lilly protested. "Not me!"

"I don't expect you to," Longarm told the woman. "I want you and Tyler to keep moving east. I want you to go to Tucson and then make arrangements to get back to Mountain City."

"And leave you?"

"Yes," Longarm told them. "I'll be along as soon as I have solved the murder and arrested the guilty party."

Tyler and Lilly exchanged quick glances and then the kid said, "It just doesn't seem right us going on to Tucson while you have to stay and face the music."

"It's my job," Longarm said. "And I can do it easier if I don't have the pair of you to worry about."

"Are you completely sure?" Lilly questioned. "Because even though I think you're crazy for not coming with us, I still have to live with my own conscience."

"I have fifty dollars in my pockets, and I could use another fifty," Longarm told her. "With that much money, I can always buy a fast horse and make tracks out of Paradise. I'd catch up with you in a day . . . two at the very most."

"All right," Lilly agreed. "I'll give you the money, and

173

we'll be on our way as soon as we bury the body."

"I'm glad that you see the sense of my plan," Longarm told her as he drove the buckboard up the faint dirt track toward the abandoned mining claim and its tailing.

In truth, he wasn't sure that any of his plan made sense. And by all rights, he probably should have stayed with the woman and the kid and helped them to reach Tucson. But the fact was Cletus Boone had been murdered, and even though the former mayor and town owner was a murderer himself, there was justice to be upheld.

So he was going to walk back into that sun-blistered little mining town, melt into the crowd and see what surprises yet awaited in Paradise.

Chapter 19

The sun was going down by the time that Longarm, some-what foot-sore and weary, approached Paradise. After they had entombed Cletus Boone in the mine, he'd spent an hour more of hard work wiping out their wagon tracks leading up to the abandoned mine. He'd made it appear as if Tyler and Lilly had stayed on the dirt road to Tucson. That way, Longarm knew that even if he were killed, his friends could not be connected to Boone's murder.

Making sure that the pair were safe had been Long-arm's primary concern, but now he intended to focus all his effort on finding Boone's killer. With that in mind, he slipped into town unnoticed and very much interested in the huge gathering of men that were milling around in front of Boone's Saloon.

"He's gone!" Aurora called from the front steps of the saloon. "My husband is gone!"

Longarm could barely see the woman, but her voice seemed to lack real grief or concern.

"Well, where the devil could he have gone?" someone yelled. "We checked all the mines and the businesses. Mayor Boone ain't been seen since he and that big mar-shal left for his office."

"I'll bet the marshal did him in!" a miner shouted.

The crowd's roar told Longarm that he was, indeed, the main murder suspect. Not that this revelation should have been surprising, since he'd publicly confronted the mayor. But he figured he had to squelch this kind of talk before it got completely out of hand.

"I didn't kill Cletus Boone," Longarm bellowed, his voice turning every head. "When I left your mayor, he was very much alive."

"Then what happened to my husband?" Aurora Boone cried.

Longarm was aware that he was treading on very thin ice because this rough, almost all male crowd was upset and wanting a victim. If he wasn't careful, they'd jump him and either beat him to death or he'd be hanged without benefit of a judge or jury.

Knowing that what he did in the next few minutes might well decide his fate, Longarm decided that this was no time for indecisiveness and marched into the crowd, shouldering men aside as he made his way up to Aurora. He yanked his badge out of his vest pocket with his left hand and his gun out of his pocket with his right. He held them both up so that his authority and determination were plainly visible to the mob.

"I'm going to find out who murdered your mayor, and then I'll take that person to the Yuma Prison."

"Oh yeah," a drunken miner shouted, waving his nearly empty bottle of whiskey. "How do we know *you* ain't the one that killed him?"

"Because I came all the way from Denver to arrest Cletus Boone. And if you don't believe me, I've got a telegram that was sent to me in Yuma that proves what I'm saying is true."

Longarm put his badge away but kept his gun in his fist as he read the telegram he'd recently received from Billy Vail telling him to arrest Boone and deliver him to the Yuma Prison. When he was finished, he said, "I mean to find out who is responsible for your mayor's disappearance."

Aurora stepped in front of him and said loud enough for everyone to hear, "And how do you plan to do that?"

"I'm going to start by questioning the folks who had the most to gain by his death and disappearance. And guess what, Mrs. Boone? You're right at the top of my suspect list. No one had more to gain than you from his death."

Aurora clawed at Longarm's eyes but he managed to knock her hands away and shout, "You're under arrest!"

A handsome but drunken man lunged forward with an upraised whiskey bottle. Longarm sidestepped the man and cracked him over the head with the barrel of his pistol. The man fell like a stone and Longarm fired a warning shot into the sky.

"Anyone who tries to interfere with this investigation will be arrested and taken to the Yuma Prison along with whoever killed your mayor. Is that clear?"

It must have been plenty clear because there was no more heckling from the crowd.

"Good," Longarm said, grabbing Aurora's arm and twisting it up behind her back. "I'll be doing my investigation out of Mayor Boone's office. And nobody had better leave town!"

"You're crazy!" Aurora hissed, struggling to break free of his grasp but failing. "I didn't kill my husband."

"We'll talk about that right now," he said, pushing her ahead and again parting the crowd.

When they were in the office, Longarm ordered, "Sit down. I'll be the one asking all the questions."

Aurora's dark eyes burned with hatred. "You can't treat people this way."

"I've got a right to question anyone I think might be guilty of murder."

"Cletus was my husband. I loved him."

"No, you didn't," Longarm said. "I doubt you even liked him."

"You *are* crazy!"

"I think you killed your husband him with a pocket

knife . . . or else paid someone else to do the dirty work. Why don't we go over to your house and have a look around? I'm sure that will turn up enough evidence to prove that you had something to do with his death."

Alarm flooded her eyes and her voice began to tremble. "You . . . you can't do that!"

"Of course I can. Furthermore, I can arrest and take you to Yuma for more questioning. I'll just bet that you aren't who you told your husband you are. You have no more royal blood than I do, and it shouldn't take more than a couple of weeks and some good investigative work to prove I'm right. You married Cletus Boone for his money, and then you either murdered him or paid a man to do it."

"Please, I . . . I didn't do it. I had nothing to do with anything. And I won't talk to you anymore. Just . . . just leave me alone and go away."

The woman had lost her composure and now Longarm was ready to play his hole card. He reached into his pocket and pulled out the murder weapon. The big jack-knife was still caked with blood, just as he'd wanted it to be when he shoved it before Aurora's lovely, lying face. Slowly unfolding the blade, he said, "Do you recognize this knife?"

"No."

"You're lying. Is it yours?"

"No! I swear it on the Holy Bible and on my mother's grave!"

"Then whose knife is it? Answer me or I swear you will rot in the Yuma Prison so long your pretty face will become as dark and wrinkled as old boot leather."

Aurora took a deep, shuddering breath. "The knife belongs to Oddie Clifton."

"Who is he?"

"He's the man you just pistol-whipped."

Longarm stared into her eyes. "Are you dead sure?"

"Of course!" she spat. "Show that knife to almost anyone in town and they'll tell you it belongs to Oddie."

"Did you hire him to kill your husband so that you could inherit all of your husband's wealth?"

"No!"

"Let's go find Oddie and wake him up," Longarm said, grabbing her arm and yanking her out of the chair. "While Oddie recovers just barely enough to speak, I'll learn the truth."

"If I could, I would kill you with my bare hands!"

"I'll keep that thought in mind," Longarm growled, propelling her back outside.

Oddie Clifton was still unconscious when Longarm and Aurora found him lying on the boardwalk surrounded by a few of his drunken friends.

One of them was bold enough to scream "What do you want with him now?"

"Some honest answers." He reached into his pocket and withdrew the murder weapon. "Is this his knife?"

The men stared and then nodded. One asked, "What's all that dark stuff on it?"

"It's Cletus Boone's blood. His throat was cut from ear to ear out behind his office in the shitter."

Their eyes widened and then they took off for the nearest saloon. Longarm hauled Oddie over to a horse watering trough. He dunked the man's head up and down so many times that he thought Oddie would drown.

But finally, Oddie coughed and his eyes opened. Longarm held the knife up before the dazed man's eyes and yelled in his face, "Is this the knife you used to slit Boone's throat?"

Oddie blinked in horror and tried to scoot away, but Longarm grabbed his shirt front and pressed the knife to his own throat hard enough to draw fresh blood. "Answer me!"

"All right! I killed him, but Aurora paid me to do it!"

Aurora screamed and, quick as a cat, she plucked Longarm's six-gun from his holster and shot Oddie right between his still unfocused eyes. Then she turned the gun on Longarm and would have killed him as well, except that a rifle blasted from an alley and Aurora stiffened, throwing back her shoulders a moment before toppling headfirst into the water trough.

Longarm half expected another bullet to take his life but, instead, Lilly and Tyler emerged from the darkness, and it was Monty Kilpatrick's son who gripped the rifle.

"She would have killed you," Tyler said quietly. "I could see right away that you were right and she wasn't any good . . . was she?"

"No," Longarm said, taking the rifle from the boy's clenched fists. "Aurora sure wasn't."

Tyler took Lilly's hand. "Please," she said, "let's just get as far away from here as we can tonight."

"I thought you and Tyler were on your way to Tucson."

"We couldn't do it," she confessed, eyes locked on the two bodies. "But I guess we can now, huh?"

A crowd was already gathering. Men were pouring into the street from every saloon. And because they were staying in Paradise until it ran out of precious ore, Longarm figured they needed to know the truth.

So he told them that Oddie had murdered their mayor, but he'd been hired and just now shot by Aurora.

Someone with the look of a merchant asked, "What do we do now that we don't have a mayor, and there's no one left that owns all the mines and businesses?"

Longarm gave the question a moment of thought, then answered, "You ought to spread the wealth around. Give everyone an equal share. You could start by electing a new mayor and an honest lawman. You could act like civilized people and make sure that it all works out fair for everyone."

They shifted on their feet and, one by one, Longarm studied their hard, dirty faces. Finally, he shook his head. "But you people won't do that. You'll fight until there are just a few left with all the wealth."

"Maybe not," the merchant said without conviction.

"Sure you will," Longarm said with resignation as he

finally located his gun in the water trough. He dried it carefully and slipped it back into his holster and then he said to Lilly and Tyler. "Let's get out of here."

"Wait a minute," someone demanded. "Why don't you think we can have elections and divvy up everything the Boone's owned fair and square?"

Longarm and his friends were already walking away.

"Marshal!" the merchant shouted, his voice filling with desperation, "I asked you a question and we all deserve an answer, dammit!"

Longarm paused for just a moment to reply, "Because none of you are angels, and this place sure as hell isn't paradise."

Watch for

**LONGARM AND THE
DESERT ROSE**

290th novel in the exciting LONGARM series
from Jove

Coming in January!

Explore the exciting Old West with one of the men who made it wild!

J. R. ROBERTS
THE GUNSMITH